At her rich, look-alike cousin's pleading, impover-ished Sacha Waverley undertakes a daring masquer-ade. She travels to Scotland posing as Lady Deirdre to care for her cousin's fiancé, the handsome, wealthy Duke of Silchester who has been temporarily blinded in a hunting accident. It's Sacha's one chance to wear fine gowns and be waited upon—a fairy-tale come true. Then the unthinkable happens...she loses her heart forever to a man she can never have.

LIGHT OF THE GODS

BARBARA CARTLAND

LIGHT OF THE GODS

Light of the Gods

First Published in United States 1982
© 1982 Barbara Cartland
This Edition Published by **Book Essentials South** 1999
Distributed by **BMI**, Ivyland, PA 18974
PRINTED IN THE UNITED STATES OF AMERICA
ISBN 1-57723-431-6

author's note

'Marriage by Consent' or 'Irregular Marriage' was completely legal in Scotland until 1949. Many people were married that way and some were trapped.

The quotations which the heroine reads to the Duke are from *The Splendours of Greece* by Robert Payne.*

This book has entranced and inspired me more than any other book on Greece and to quote Robert Payne:

"The splendour of Greece still lights our skies, reaching over America and Asia and lands which the Greeks never dreamed existed. There would be no Christianity as we know it without the fertilizing influence of the Greek Fathers of the Church, who owed their training to Greek philosophy ... we owe to the Greeks the beginning of Science and the beginning of thought. They built the greatest Temples ever made, carved marble with delicacy and skill, and set in motion the questioning mind which refuses to believe there are any bounds to reason."

chapter one

1860

SACHA was arranging the flowers in the Sitting-Room when she heard the sound of wheels outside the front door.

As Nanny who looked after her and her father were out, she quickly put down the flowers she was holding to smooth down her gown and took a quick look in the mirror over the mantelpiece to see whether her hair was tidy.

As she had been busy all the morning with household chores in the Vicarage she had not been concerned with her appearance, and she hoped now that whoever had arrived, presumably to see her father, would not be anybody of importance.

At the same time there were few people in the Parish who drove in carriages.

The farmers had high wooden carts and the Doctor drove a gig in the summer to which, in the winter, was added an aged leather hood which gave him some protection against the weather.

Whoever it was had stopped at the front door and there was a rat-tat on the knocker.

Sacha hurried from the Sitting-Room and saw to her astonishment coming through the open door a vision in pale pink who looked like a flower from the garden.

"Deirdre!" she exclaimed.

"Good morning, Sacha!" her cousin Lady Deirdre Lang replied. "I expect you are surprised to see me!"

"Very surprised!" Sacha agreed. "I thought you were in London."

"I was, but I returned home the night before last."

Deirdre walked into the Sitting-Room ahead of Sacha and looked around it rather disdainfully before she said:

"Shut the door. I want to talk to you."

Sacha looked at her questioningly.

Deirdre was her first cousin and they were almost exactly the same age, but since they had grown up she had found the closeness they had enjoyed as children had vanished.

Instead, when Deirdre came to see her, which was not very often, she always felt uncomfortably aware that she was the poor relation and both Deirdre and her parents despised her father.

It had been different when her mother was alive, but she had died three years ago, and since then Sacha was very aware of how unimportant the daughter of the Vicar of Little Langsworth was, except that the patron of his living was her Uncle, the Marquess of Langsworth.

When Lady Margaret Lang, the only daughter of the second Marquess, had insisted against strong paternal opposition on marrying the Reverend Mervyn Waverley, her relations had metaphorically 'washed their hands' of her.

"How can you be so foolish as to waste your looks and your position in life on a Curate?" they had asked.

They had not listened when Lady Margaret replied she was 'head over heels in love' with the best looking, the most charming and the most attractive man she had ever met.

It was not surprising that they did not believe her, because Lady Margaret had been a great social success in London and had a number of suitors for her hand.

In fact, her father was considering whether to accept a very distinguished Peer, or a Baronet whose income and estates far exceeded his own.

But Lady Margaret had said that either she must be allowed to marry the man she loved, or she would run away with him, which would undoubtedly cause a scandal.

After months of argument, tears and pleadings which Lady Margaret ignored, her father had capitulated.

She was married quietly with no congratulations and few presents, and two blissfully happy people settled down outside her father's Park-Gates, in the small Vicarage, which fortunately had just become empty.

The old Vicar, who was over eighty, had died and the Marquess thought the least he could do for his daughter was to provide her with a roof over her head, and her husband with a living.

He was not however very generous as regards the stipend of his new son-in-law. Nevertheless the bride and bridegroom were too happy to concern themselves with anything except each other, and had no wish to see their relatives or be entertained by them.

It was only some years later that Lady Margaret realised she was depriving her daughter of many pleasures that should be hers by right, and as her brother had now become the third Marquess his daughter and Sacha shared a Governess.

This meant as far as Sacha was concerned that she could enjoy many luxuries she would otherwise have missed.

There was a magnificent early Georgian house to roam over, a superlative Library filled with books for her to read, and a stable full of horses which she could ride with Deirdre.

The new Marchioness however followed the attitude of her predecessors in thinking that Lady Margaret had made a fool of herself, and took every opportunity to make her aware of it.

"Whenever I sing: 'The rich man in his Castle, the poor man at his gate, God made them high or lowly,'" Margaret Waverley once said to her husband, "I am thinking of Alice who is so very conscious that God made her 'high' when we chose to be 'lowly.'"

Her husband laughed, but he had said:

"If it really upsets you, my darling, I will ask for a transfer to another parish. I am sure the Bishop will be sympathetic and provide me with another living, if I ask him urgently."

"No, of course not!" Lady Margaret replied. "Anyway if we went away, Sacha would have none of the advantages she has now, for you know perfectly well we cannot afford the sort of horses she rides, or the teachers she enjoys with Deirdre."

She knew if she was honest that it was Sacha who enjoyed most the music lessons the girls had from a very

4

experienced teacher who had been a professional musician until his health broke down.

It was Sacha who really loved the dancing lessons which took place in the Ball-Room of the Castle, in order that Deirdre when she went to London could learn to dance at all the smartest Balls with a grace that she did not have naturally.

It was Sacha too who was very grateful for the books in the Library, and was really the only person in the house who made full use of them.

"Do you know, Papa," she had said to her father when she was fifteen, "the Curator told me today that I am the only person who has ever taken a volume from the Greek shelf, and there are a large number that you do not have here."

Her father had looked interested.

"I wonder if they would be useful for the translations I am doing?" he questioned.

"I will write their titles down for you, Papa," Sacha said, "or better still, bring them home for you to have a look at."

There was a little pause before the Vicar replied:

"I am not sure we should borrow books without the permission of your Uncle, and quite frankly I am not very keen at the moment to ask any favours of him."

Sacha smiled.

She knew her father was having a disagreement with his brother-in-law over the condition of some of the cottages in which the old pensioners were living.

In spite of his great wealth, the Marquess could be very cheese-paring over things that did not concern him personally, and her father had pointed out firmly that some of the older pensioners were suffering in their health

5

as a result of roofs that leaked and windows that did not fit.

"It is all right, Papa," Sacha said. "Mr. Cornwall the Curator is so thrilled that I am as interested in the books as he is, that he will let me borrow anything I want."

She did not listen to her father's protests but brought back any of the books in Greek which she knew would help his studies.

The Vicar had in the last five years started to supplement their very inadequate income by writing books, mostly translations from the Greek which had a small sale amongst scholars and University Libraries.

Nevertheless, as Lady Margaret had said, 'every little bit helped,' and she was also exceedingly proud that her husband was acclaimed by intellectuals as being an authority on Ancient Greece.

At Langsworth Hall however, they were interested only in the Social World in which as soon as she was a débutante, Deirdre shone brilliantly.

She was not only exceedingly pretty with the beauty of an English rose, but was dressed by the most expensive dressmakers in London and entertained for on a grandiose scale at Langsworth House in Berkeley Square. So it was not surprising that she was acclaimed and courted.

To Sacha her emergence from the School-Room had changed her life overnight.

There was no longer the daily visit to the Hall. The lessons which she had enjoyed while Deirdre grumbled about them stopped automatically, as did her dancing and her riding.

Even more to be regretted, it was now difficult to borrow books from the Library. While Mr. Cornwall would be only too pleased to see her, she was well aware that if she met her Aunt she would ask for an explanation of her presence in a way which would make it very clear she was an interloper in the house.

Now that Deirdre was grown up Sacha was expected to keep her place in the village.

Without her mother's support it was impossible for her to do anything but try to forget all the delights she had enjoyed at Langsworth Hall and just be grateful for the years they had been available to her.

Fortunately there was a great deal for her to do at home.

With Lady Margaret's death, the small allowance she had received from the Langsworth Estate came to an end, and Sacha and her father had to live entirely on his stipend and the proceeds from his books.

This meant they could no longer afford any extra help in the house and what Nanny, who was getting on in years, could not do, fell on Sacha's shoulders.

She was always happy to be with her father and was perfectly content to sit talking to him in the evenings.

That they were both busy during the day made the hours slip by quickly until they could enter into one of their spirited discussions on historical subjects that inevitably ended up in their talking about the Greeks.

Her father's knowledge of the Ancient Greeks and of the gods and goddesses they worshipped was so fascinating to Sacha that she could never hear enough about them.

She also tried to help him with his translations, sometimes surprisingly finding the best English equivalent of a word more quickly than he did.

It was however a very restricting life for a young girl, especially one as lovely as Sacha was at eighteen.

"If you ask me, Vicar," Nanny had said to him bluntly a few days ago, "it's a crying shame that His Lordship doesn't do something for his niece, seeing as how she and Lady Deirdre was so close when they was children."

The Vicar looked up from his desk to ask a little vaguely:

"What do you mean by 'something,' Nanny?"

"I means, Sir, that it would be only right for Miss Sacha to go to a few Balls an' meet gentlemen who'd admire her in the same way as they admires Lady Deirdre. There's not much difference between them, seeing as how Miss Sacha is the living spit of her mother, and Lady Deirdre takes after her father. They might almost be twins."

"I suppose there is a resemblance," the Vicar agreed.

"There would be, if Miss Sacha had one decent gown to wear, instead of those cheap cottons which are the best I can make her."

After a pause the Vicar said:

"You know, Nanny, we cannot afford at the moment to spend any money on clothes."

"I know that, Sir," Nanny replied, "and even if you bought Miss Sacha a gown from Bond Street, where could she wear it, except to dazzle the sprouts and cabbages and the few villagers who come to Church on a Sunday?"

The Vicar did not reply, and after a moment Nanny said:

"It's a crying shame that pretty child is slaving away here and never asked to any of the entertainments taking place up at the Big House. I'm sure if Her Ladyship was alive she'd have something to say about it and I only wish I could give His Lordship a piece of my mind!"

As Nanny finished speaking she flounced out of the Study door and shut it sharply behind her.

The Vicar sighed.

He knew only too well that what Nanny was saying was true, but there was nothing he could do.

He would not go down on his knees to his brother-in-law to beg him to invite Sacha to the house-parties which took place regularly at what the village people called the 'Big House.'

He knew moreover only too well there was not a chance in a million of Deirdre inviting Sacha to accompany her to London during the Season.

He looked at the miniature of his wife that was standing on his desk and wondered if her eyes were reproaching him.

"What can I do, dearest?" he asked in his heart. "This is another reason why I miss you unbearably and find myself lost because you are not here."

However much his religion told him they would meet again in another world, the Vicar knew he wanted his wife with him now.

The aching void she had left when she died seemed to grow more painful as the years passed and every moment of every day he missed her more and more agonisingly.

When Nanny said more or less the same thing to Sacha she merely laughed.

"Can you imagine Deirdre inviting me to her parties?" she asked. "You know as well as I do she is ashamed of me because I am so unimportant."

"Jealous, more like!" Nanny replied abruptly.

Sacha laughed again.

"Dearest Nanny, you know that Her Ladyship has nothing to be jealous about where I am concerned."

Even while she spoke she knew that was not quite true. Deirdre had always been jealous of everything that anybody else had, which might be hers.

She had hated the High Sheriff's daughter because she had an adoring young man who followed her in the Hunting-Field and who danced with nobody else at the parties which had been given for them before they were grown up.

Sacha used to be invited to these, and because she had enjoyed herself and looked so pretty as she did so Deirdre had been very unpleasant to her as they drove home from the last one they had been to together.

"I thought you made an exhibition of yourself, Sacha, when you were dancing *Oranges and Lemons,*" she said, "and you must have persuaded the boys in some underhand way to give you so many favours in the *Cotillion.*"

"You had more than anybody else," Sacha said, hoping to appease her.

"Considering I had the prettiest dress in the room, I ought to have had them all," Deirdre replied.

The Marchioness had joined in:

"That is true, my dearest, and you shall have another gown from Madame Yvonne although she is very expensive."

Because she was determined to make Sacha feel small she added:

"You might suggest to your mother, Sacha, that you have a new gown. The one you are wearing is too tight, and in my opinion too short."

"I will tell Mama, Aunt Alice," Sacha replied meekly.

She knew that her gown was in fact just right, and her aunt was only being unpleasant because Deirdre was jealous of her.

Now for the last year she had not seen Deirdre, and had only heard about her from the talk in the village.

Because most of the servants up at the Big House came from the Little Langsworth the stories of Deirdre's success in the Social World was passed from mouth to mouth, and there was very little that went on either in London or in the country that Sacha did not learn.

She was aware that a number of distinguished gentlemen had proposed to her cousin, that the Queen had given her a special smile when she was presented at Buckingham Palace, and that there were whispers of an impending marriage to somebody of very great importance.

Sacha had found it all fascinating, although sometimes she thought a little wistfully that it would be delightful to see Deirdre herself and hear from her what was happening.

Now astonishingly, when she least expected it, Deirdre had appeared and instead of sending for her had actually come to the Vicarage.

Because she could not help it she said impulsively:

"You look lovely, Deirdre! I have never seen you in pink before, and it makes you look very, very beautiful!"

"That is what everybody says," Deirdre answered complacently, "but I am not certain I do not look better in blue."

She walked to the mantelpiece as she spoke to look at her reflection in the mirror as Sacha had done.

"The other night," she said, "I wore pale green at a Ball given at Buckingham Palace, and I heard afterwards that the Prince Consort said it was the prettiest gown in the room!"

"Oh, Deirdre, how wonderful for you! Did you dance every dance?"

"Of course!" Deirdre replied. "And a number of very distinguished gentlemen were extremely annoyed when they found my programme was filled and they were unable therefore to have even one dance with me."

"I am sure you are the Belle of every Ball you attend."

"Of course I am," Deirdre said turning from the mirror, "and I have come to tell you, Sacha, a secret which you must not repeat to anybody."

"You know if you tell me something in confidence I will be as silent as the grave!" Sacha promised.

She thought excitedly that with Deirdre confiding in her it was just like old times when they shared special secrets which must not be revealed to their parents.

"Do sit down, dearest," she said indicating the sofa, "and tell me why you have come to see me. I have missed you more than I can possibly say."

Just for a moment Deirdre had the grace to look embarrassed. Then she said:

"I have been so busy, Sacha! I was saying to Mama only yesterday that I never have a moment to myself."

"I understand, of course I understand," Sacha said. "And now you are here you have a secret to tell me?"

Deirdre lowered her voice.

"The secret is that I am to become engaged to the Duke of Silchester!"

Sacha looked at her wide-eyed.

"How exciting! How wonderful for you! Do you love him very much?"

"I am delighted that I should marry the Duke. Think of it, Sacha, I shall be a Duchess and walk into dinner before Mama!"

"Tell me about him," Sacha begged. "Is he very handsome?"

"Yes, very, and it so like you Sacha, not to have heard of him. He is one of the most important Dukes in England, a big race-horse owner, and has an enormous house in Buckinghamshire, far, far bigger than ours!"

"It sounds everything you should have," Sacha cried. "When are you to be married?"

There was a little pause. Then Deirdre replied:

"Papa is making all the arrangements, and we are first to have an engagement party to which all our relatives will be invited, and of course, everybody of importance in the County."

"When will that be?" Sacha enquired.

"In about three week's time, but Papa says nobody is to know that we are engaged until then because it would spoil the surprise."

"I am so glad you have told me," Sacha said, "and you know, Deirdre, I shall pray that you will be marvellously happy."

Deirdre did not answer, and after a moment Sacha said:

"What is wrong?"

"There is nothing wrong," Deirdre replied. "It is just that I need your help."

"My help?"

"Yes, Sacha. You can help me, and it is something you must do."

"But of course!" Sacha said. "I will do anything you ask of me, as I always have, Deirdre."

"That is what I knew you would say," Deirdre replied. "Now listen carefully, because this is important."

Sacha had sat down beside her cousin on the sofa, and now Deirdre turned to her to say:

"Papa heard the day before yesterday that the Duke has had an accident!"

"An accident? Was he injured?"

Deirdre nodded.

"He is in Scotland with his grandmother, and he stood on a gun-trap."

"Oh, no!" Sacha exclaimed. "How terrible!"

She was well aware that gun-traps were dangerous because her father often deplored the use of them in the same way that he thought man-traps were hideous instruments of cruelty.

He had explained to Sacha that gun-traps were used in the North of England and Scotland, and less commonly in the South, to catch foxes and wild-cats which preyed on sporting birds.

A small animal such as a rabbit, or sometimes a lamb, was put alive in the trap, and when a fox, attracted by its bleating, went to investigate the trap, it exploded either killing it or inflicting serious wounds.

"They are barbarously inhuman!" the Vicar had said angrily. "Nobody should use such contraptions."

He was angry because he suspected that one of the Marquess's keepers had been using a gun-trap not only to trap and kill foxes but also to warn poachers that their lives could be in danger.

He had been successful in having both gun-traps and man-traps abolished on the Langsworth Estate, but not before there had been some rather heated arguments with the Marquess.

"You must be very upset about the Duke," Sacha said a little breathlessly.

"I am sorry for him," Deirdre answered, "but at the same time, I have no wish to go to Scotland."

"Has he asked you to go to him?"

"His grandmother has written to Papa saying that as he is very depressed being confined to bed and having to be operated on to remove the pieces of metal which were driven into his body by the explosion, it would be a nice gesture on my part if I went North to stay with her at her Castle."

"It is a long journey," Sacha said, "but I am sure you will want to go."

There was silence before Deirdre said:

"That is just the point, Sacha. I do not want to go and in fact I cannot go at the moment!"

"Why not?"

"Because Lord Gerard has already invited me to a party he is giving specially for me at his house which is about thirty miles from here. Having accepted his invitation, I have no intention of letting him down."

"But Deirdre, surely if you are going to marry the Duke you will want to be with him when he needs you?"

Deirdre seemed to be feeling for words before she said:

"That is not the point. Lord Gerard is a—close friend, and this party has been planned for some time. He is giving a small dance, very intimate and cosy, and there will be lots of fascinating things to do in the daytime. I have to go, and what is more, I intend to do so!"

There was a hard note in Deirdre's voice which Sacha did not miss. Then because she was very perceptive and knew Deirdre so well, she said:

"I think, dearest, Lord Gerard means something very . . . special to . . . you."

For a moment she thought Deirdre was going to deny it. Then she said:

"I am very fond of him, and I want to go to his party."

Sacha's eyes were searching her cousin's face. Then she said:

"Deirdre, you love him! Why do you not marry him?"

"How can I when the Duke has asked me?" Deirdre objected. "Papa and Mama are so thrilled that I shall be a Duchess! Think of the position I shall hold at Court, as well as in the country at the Duke's ancestral home and at all the other houses he owns!"

Deirdre drew in her breath before she went on:

"And the Silchester diamonds are famous! There is

a tiara that looks just like a crown!"

"But you love Lord Gerard!"

"There is no use in going on saying that!" Deirdre answered irritably. "And even if I do, it would be crazy and would infuriate Papa and Mama if I refused the Duke. No—I have every intention of marrying him, but I am going to Harry's party because it will be the last time I will be able to see him before I am married."

There was almost a little sob in Deirdre's voice and Sacha put out her hand to lay it on hers.

"Do you really think, dearest, however important you are you will be happy with the Duke when you love somebody else? Will you not find yourself always regretting that you have given up Lord Gerard when he might have been your husband?"

"He cannot offer me enough," Deirdre replied, "and that is the truth. His estate is small and I know he is in debt, but I want to be rich—very rich, and a Duchess!"

Sacha wanted to say that her mother had married her father and never regretted it for one moment, but she knew Deirdre would not believe that, just as in the past she had often asked:

"How could your mother give up living here for that pokey little Vicarage?"

"I have known nobody as happy as Papa and Mama are together," Sacha had answered loyally.

"Well, I think it was sheer madness on your mother's part," Deirdre answered. "I am sure sometimes she longs for pretty clothes, for carriages, horses, servants, and of course the company of distinguished and important people who certainly do not find the Vicarage amusing."

There was no use, Sacha thought, in using her mother as an example of what her cousin should do now. At the same time, she was sure that Deirdre was making a mistake that she would regret bitterly in the years ahead.

"Of course, I have quite a lot of money of my own," Deirdre said as if she was following the train of her own thoughts, "but I have no intention of spending it on a man, when I expect him to spend his money on me!"

"When you marry," Sacha replied, "it is the law that a woman's property becomes her husband's. So you will not feel it is yours any longer."

"I should!" Deirdre asserted. "Anyway, even then I should want more, and the Duke is very rich."

Sacha clasped her hands together.

"Oh, Deirdre, do think about this sensibly. I want you to be happy. I want you to find real love, and I have always been afraid in my heart that you might be forced into an arranged marriage."

"That is exactly what this is," Deirdre replied, "and very much to my advantage. Stop being foolish, Sacha. I am going to marry the Duke, and I shall enjoy it very much, but I also intend to go to Harry's party, and that is where you have to help me."

"How?" Sacha asked bewildered. "What can I do?"

Deirdre paused before she said slowly:

"You are going to Scotland in my place, to make yourself pleasant to the ailing Duke!"

"That is ridiculous!" Sacha explained in horrified tones. "He does not want to see me, he wants you."

"That is who he will think he is getting."

There was silence. Then Sacha said:

"I do not...understand! Explain to me what you are...saying."

"You are being very stupid!" Deirdre said impatiently. "It is quite simple: I am going to Harry's party while you travel to Scotland, pretending to be me, to stay with the Duke's grandmother, and soothe his fevered brow, or whatever one does when a man is ill."

"I think you have gone mad!" Sacha said. "Are you seriously suggesting that the Duke would believe I was you?"

"Oh, I forgot to tell you," Deirdre said airily. "At the moment he is blind!"

"Blind?"

"Yes, the explosion from the gun-trap affected his eyes. His grandmother said in her letter to Papa that they hoped it was only a temporary affliction, but they could not be sure until the bandages were removed."

"How awful! How terrible!" Sacha said. "I can hardly believe it!"

"It is true," Deirdre replied, "and that is why, dearest Sacha, the Duke will assuredly think it is I who is sitting beside him and commiserating with him over his accident, while I shall be enjoying myself in a very different manner."

"And you really believe he will think I am you?"

"Why not?"

"But there will be other people . . . his grandmother . . . the servants . . ."

"They have never seen me," Deirdre answered. "We have always been told that we look so alike, that we might easily be sisters, or even twins."

"You are much, much more beautiful than I am ever likely to be," Sacha said.

"That is true," Deirdre agreed. "At the same time if you were dressed like me and your hair was done in the latest fashion there would be no reason for anybody to doubt that you were who you purported to be."

"Of course they would!"

"Now listen," Deirdre went on, "and stop making idiotic remarks. Papa and Mama are going to stay at

Windsor with the Queen for an Agricultural Show, or something that is taking place there, as they are driving there very early tomorrow morning."

She was silent before she said:

"You and I will leave an hour later for the station where we will be seen off by Papa's secretary, Mr. Webster. I shall however, leave the train at the first stop where Harry will be waiting for me."

Sacha gave a little cry.

"But, Deirdre, supposing someone sees you?"

"Why should anyone? Besides they will see *'me'* as they think, carried on in the train to London!"

"It is too complicated! I shall never be able to do it!"

"I have thought it all out very carefully," Deirdre said, "or rather Harry has, and all you have to do is to follow our instructions."

"What . . . will happen when I . . . get to London?"

"You will be met by the Clerk who works under Mr. Webster. He has already left for London, and as he is new, he has never seen me except perhaps in the distance."

"What is his name?"

"Evans. He will have reserved a carriage for you on the Scottish Express and will take you to the train. Harry says that fortunately there is just time for you to change stations without going to our house in Berkeley Square."

Because she was too bewildered to say anything Sacha just stared at Deirdre as she went on:

"You cannot travel alone of course, and I must take Hannah with me because I want to look my best for Harry's party. But you can have Emily to accompany you. She is half-witted, but she will do exactly as she is told."

"But surely she might talk?" Sacha said.

Deirdre shook her head.

"I have had to let Hannah into my secret. You know as she dotes on me she will do anything I want, so she will tell Emily that if she ever breathes to any living soul what has happened, she will be dismissed without a reference, and will never again be employed in a decent household."

Deirdre paused for breath. Then she continued:

"Hannah is, at the moment, sorting out all my old clothes which you can have, and there is a whole pile of them which I might have given you before if I had thought about it. They are cluttering up every wardrobe, and I have to dispose of them so as to make room for my new trousseau."

She gave a cry of rapture as she added:

"Oh, Sacha, if you only knew the wonderful gowns I am going to have as a bride! Every woman who sees them will die of envy!"

Sacha found her voice.

"But Deirdre . . . we cannot do . . . this! I shall be . . . exposed and let you down . . . and you will never . . . forgive me."

."That is true," Deirdre replied, "if you dared to do such a thing! But if you behave cautiously there is no reason why anybody should be in the least suspicious. As I was saying, we are so alike that people will accept you without question."

She gave a little laugh as she said:

"Do you remember that teacher we had who always used to say to us: 'People see what they expect to see?' And when we experimented on the servants and on Papa and Mama, we found it was absolutely true! They remembered what they had thought they had seen, but actually it was something quite different."

"It is rather . . . different for you and me."

"There is no difference!" Deirdre contradicted. "And Sacha, I cannot believe that after all these years you would refuse to help me when I am begging you to do so."

Now there was a genuine appeal in Deirdre's voice and Sacha answered meekly:

"Is . . . is the Duke really . . . blind?"

"There would have been no reason for his grandmother to say so if he was not. In fact, she is very upset about it."

"He will be upset if he finds out you have . . . deceived him. Does he not love you . . . very, very . . . much?"

"Of course he does!" Deirdre answered. "He told me I was the most beautiful girl he had ever seen! At the same time he is nearly thirty, and he should have had an heir long ago."

"He . . . sounds rather . . . frightening!"

"I am not frightened of anybody," Deirdre retorted, "but of course Talbot, that is his name, is very conscious of his own importance, and he obviously had to marry somebody who was his equal in the Social World."

She preened herself before she added:

"He will find nobody better equipped than I am to look beautiful at the end of his table and to grace the Silchester diamonds."

"How could he!" Sacha exclaimed, "and that is why . . ."

"You are not going to argue with me, dear, dear Sacha? You know you love me, and you know you want to help me. Just say 'yes' quickly, because we have a lot to do."

Sacha looked at Deirdre enquiringly and she explained:

"First of all we have to see Hannah has the trunks ready to take with you, then we must choose what you will wear in which to travel. First impressions are always important! I must also give you some money for tips and incidentals."

"You know I have never . . . travelled very far . . . alone," Sacha said in a frightened voice:

"I know that," Deirdre replied, "but once Mr. Evans has put you on the Express, all you have to do is to sit there until you arrive."

Sacha gave a sigh.

"I am glad there is somebody to take me and Emily across London. It would be disastrous if I lost myself."

"You will have to be more self-sufficient in the future," Deirdre said sternly. "After all, we are grown up now, Sacha."

"Yes, I know," Sacha agreed humbly, "but you have done so much more than I have."

Then she gave a sudden cry.

"What about Papa?"

"Oh, really!" Deirdre exclaimed. "Do I have to think of everything? That is quite easy! You will tell your father that I have asked you to come with me to Scotland. He is not likely to refuse to allow you to accompany me on such a long journey, when I am worried about my future husband's health."

"Yes . . . I suppose so."

"Very well, then, it is all settled," Deirdre said. "Put on your bonnet and come with me to the Hall, and see the clothes I am going to give you. Then be ready for me to pick you up tomorrow morning."

Sacha drew in her breath.

"I can hardly . . . believe that I have agreed to do this."

Then she laughed.

"It was always I in the past who thought of mad things to do which got us into a great deal of trouble with our Governesses. Now the tables are turned, and this time it is you, Deirdre, who has thought out something so astonishing and so dramatic that I just cannot believe it is real."

"It is real to me, and I am determined to be with Harry. I cannot imagine anything that would bore me more than sitting talking to a man who is not only ill— but blind!"

"But... surely you feel very... very sorry for him?"

"I suppose so, but his silly old grandmother should not have gun-traps on her estate, and he should not have been so foolish as to walk into one!"

"I hope that is not what you expect me to say to him!" Sacha teased.

Deirdre laughed.

"No, indeed. You have to be a ministering angel and tell him that he will soon be well and look as handsome as he did before."

"Is that the sort of thing you say?" Sacha asked.

"Good gracious, no!" Deirdre replied. "I expect men to tell me how beautiful, wonderful, and of course, adorable I am!"

She fluttered her long dark eye-lashes against her cheeks as she said:

"Men like a woman to be simpering and coy, because it makes them feel big, strong and masculine, but sometimes I want to laugh in their faces for being so stupid."

"Stupid?"

"In thinking that women are not sharp enough to see through a lot of their pretensions, and many of their conceits.".

She smiled complacently as she added:

"You know, Sacha, when you used to bully me into doing my lessons with you I never realised then what a great advantage it is to have brains. Some of the girls I met in London were so stupid that they made fools of themselves over the simplest things."

She raised her chin to say:

"Thank goodness I am clever, and the way I have thought out this plan is very good proof of it!"

Sacha felt rather guilty as she remembered that in the past she had thought Deirdre very stupid when it came to lessons. She never read a book if she could help it, and spoke no languages except for a smattering of French.

Then she realised that Deirdre was not talking about academic knowledge, but about being quick-witted and able to turn anything that happened to its best advantage for herself.

That she had always been very good at doing, and Sacha could see only too clearly how this tangled plot had emerged simply because she intended to go to Lord Gerard's party and had no consideration for the Duke whom she was to marry.

"It is unkind of me to think such things," she told herself. At the same time she knew that was true.

Deirdre jumped to her feet.

"Come along, Sacha," she said. "There is no time to be wasted and the carriage is outside. Tell your maid you will be having luncheon with me, and you can make all the explanations to your father later this evening."

"Yes . . . of course."

Deirdre walked out of the Sitting-Room and across the Hall as Sacha ran upstairs to put on her bonnet. It was the only decent one she possessed, but it was two years old and had been retrimmed twice.

As she put it on thinking how drab she would look beside Deirdre in her pink gown with her flower-trimmed bonnet, she remembered there were clothes waiting for her at the Big House.

'It will be lovely to have them,' she thought to herself, 'but perhaps I am wrong to agree to this ... crazy masquerade.'

Then she knew she really had little choice in the matter.

Deirdre had made up her mind and if she opposed her Sacha was certain she would not only be very disagreeable about it, but would somehow avenge herself not only on her, but on her father.

There had been so many difficulties in one way or another between the Vicar and the Marquess. Sacha had often been afraid that her father in speaking up for what he believed was right and Christian would antagonise his brother-in-law, to the point where he would be turned out of the living.

The Marquess then might use his influence with the Bishop to ensure that the Reverend Mervyn Waverley was on the black-list and considered unemployable.

Sacha assured herself that this would not happen, but at the same time she was sensible enough to realise that it *could* occur, and their safe, secure little world would crumble overnight.

She had often told herself that it was her job to look after her father now that her mother was no longer there.

But she knew because he was very direct and very outspoken, when he was defending his Parishioners, that she had to curb him and soften his attitude rather than accentuate it.

As she ran down the stairs to tell Nanny that she was going to the Big House with Deirdre she found herself saying a little prayer to her mother.

"I know you will not approve, Mama," she said, "but I do not see there is anything else I can do. Please . . . please help me and make sure that nobody guesses that I am an . . . imposter."

chapter two

WHEN Deirdre jumped out of the train almost before it had stopped at the station, she hardly bothered to say goodbye, but Sacha had a glimpse of a smartly dressed very good-looking man, who was meeting her.

When the train started off again Sacha could hardly believe that she was setting off alone on what she knew was a crazy adventure.

Ever since Deirdre had forced her to agree to take her place in Scotland with the Duke she had felt as if she was living in a dream and at any moment might wake up.

They had driven back to Langsworth Hall and when Sacha saw the clothes that Hannah was packing for her into two huge leather trunks, she could hardly believe that they were to be hers.

"You cannot give me so much!" she had cried.

"I have no further use for them," Deirdre replied, "and Hannah has been complaining for a long time that there is no room in the wardrobes."

"That's true enough, M'Lady," Hannah said, "and I'm sure Miss Sacha will be able to make good use of them!"

She gave a disparaging glance as she spoke at the gown Sacha was wearing and as if she knew what she was thinking Deirdre said:

"Now we have to decide, Hannah, and it is important, what Miss Sacha should wear for the journey. As I have already said to her, first impressions are important."

Hannah's lips tightened, and Sacha was aware without her saying anything that she disapproved of the whole idea of her going to Scotland in Deirdre's place.

She sympathised because she disapproved of it herself and thought she was making a terrible mistake which might have disastrous consequences.

She knew however, it was useless to ask Deirdre to think of some other plan, because she remembered that in the past once her cousin had made up her mind she was as ruthless and determined as any man.

A long discussion followed between Deirdre and Hannah in which Sacha took no part, and finally a travelling-gown in hyacinth blue was produced with a cape to cover it, which was trimmed with satin of the same colour and was very attractive.

The crinoline had grown so large in the last few years that Sacha had said laughingly:

"It is a good thing I can only afford to wear a very small one, otherwise I would never be able to get inside the Vicarage!"

The cages of Deirdre's crinolines seemed enormous,

and she thought another problem might be that she would not be able to handle them competently.

There were all sorts of amusing cartoons in the newspapers and magazines showing women floating up into the air because the wind had got under their crinolines or being obviously very indecent if they bent over and their skirts tipped upwards.

But Sacha was aware that anything she said would be disregarded, and she therefore accepted gratefully the beautiful travelling-gown and everything that went with it.

There was a bonnet trimmed with tiny ostrich feathers, gloves, a handbag, and shoes that luckily fitted her because she and Deirdre were the same size.

She was slightly thinner round the waist which annoyed her cousin, but Hannah said the seamstress would alter as many gowns as she could before the trunks came down to the Vicarage late that evening.

"I will do the rest when they arrive," Sacha said eagerly, "and of course Nanny will help me."

She thought as she spoke that Nanny would certainly be stunned at Deirdre's sudden and unexpected generosity, for she had often said:

"I can't think why Her Ladyship isn't generous enough to send you one of her old gowns occasionally. But there, she always was selfish from the time she was in the cradle!"

"I expect she is so busy and has so much to do now, Nanny, that she has forgotten me," Sacha replied.

Nanny was not placated by the soft answer, and when the trunks arrived at the Vicarage, besides four large hat-boxes and an expensively fitted dressing-case, Nanny had looked at them and said:

"Now what's Her Ladyship up to, I wonder, that she's

being so open-handed suddenly?"

Sacha was aware that this was dangerous ground, and she said quickly:

"I cannot think why you should suspect that Lady Deirdre is up to anything, Nanny. After all, we always shared things when we were children."

"There's not been much sharing here this last year since Her Ladyship became a success in London," Nanny snapped.

As that was unanswerable Sacha did not reply.

Her father, as she had expected, accepted with pleasure the story that she was to travel with Deirdre to Scotland because he thought it would be a change for her.

"I can quite understand Deirdre does not want to make that long journey alone, my darling," he said. "And I am sorry to learn of the Duke's accident. He is a great sportsman."

"I have never heard you mention him, Papa."

The Vicar smiled.

"I find myself more interested in Greek gods and goddesses than in English Dukes. At the same time Silchester's horse won the Derby last year, and as a number of my Parishoners risked their money on him, I was extremely gratified when he won."

Sacha smiled and added:

"Otherwise the Sunday collection would have been sadly depleted!"

"Of course," the Vicar agreed. "If people have what they call 'bad luck' they usually blame their prayers for not being effective, and not their own stupidity."

"I shall not be away for long, Papa," Sacha said thankfully.

Deirdre had told her she was to stay for exactly a

week, then take a train which would enable them to meet at the station where they had left each other, so that they could arrive back in the village together.

"Are you telling your father and mother," Sacha asked, "that I am going with you?"

"No, of course not," Deirdre replied. "Papa might mention it in a letter to the Dowager Duchess, and that would be disastrous. No, the only person who knows that story is your father, and of course Harry. And I must drop you at the Vicarage when we return, otherwise your father might ask embarrassing questions."

Sacha was thankful that Deirdre accepted that whatever she might do, they could not ask the Vicar to tell a lie!

If he knew the truth he would undoubtedly think that it was wicked to be so deceitful and would forbid her to impersonate her cousin.

The night before she left Sacha had lain awake worrying and wishing she was strong enough to refuse to do what Dierdre asked.

But once she was alone on the journey with Emily, she began to feel excited because it was so different from anything she had done before.

The reserved carriage was, she thought, like a little house they had all to themselves, but she knew that Emily was frightened of the train and was watching apprehensively the country slipping past the windows as if she thought at any moment they might be involved in an accident.

She was, as Deirdre had said, a rather stupid girl who had come from the village to work in the Big House, and had risen from being the lowliest and most unimportant house-maid to become assistant to Hannah.

Her job, Sacha knew, was to do everything Hannah

ordered, which included all the unpleasant tasks that the elderly maid did not wish to do herself.

Emily looked very respectable in her black dress with a shawl over her shoulders, and was wearing black cotton gloves and thick-soled sensible leather shoes.

"We have a long journey in front of us," Sacha said, thinking she should speak to Emily now they were alone.

"Yes, Miss."

"We shall not arrive at the Castle until tomorrow afternoon. It will be very interesting to see the countryside as we pass through it."

"Yes, Miss."

Sacha thought there was no point in continuing the conversation, and like Emily she looked out at the countryside.

At the same time she was thinking of Deirdre and how she had obviously been excited just before the train drew up at the station where she was to meet Lord Gerard.

"Why can she not be brave enough to marry the man she loves?" Sacha wondered. "After all, it is not as if Lord Gerard is a poor Curate as Papa was."

She assumed that since he had taken all this trouble he was very much in love with Deirdre.

"How can he help it, when she is so beautiful?" Sacha asked herself.

At the same time she knew if she was honest that Deirdre would be a very selfish wife, very different from her mother, who adored her father and made everything, even the privations they had to endure, fun because she was so happy.

The Vicarage had always seemed to be filled with laughter and Lady Margaret had radiated the love that was in her heart so that she seemed to infect everybody with whom she came in contact.

When she died the Parishioners had mourned her in a way that was very touching and almost as if she was one of their own relatives.

At the Funeral Sacha had been surprised to see people from all parts of the County who had turned to her mother in trouble and whom she had helped and comforted.

There were representatives from most of the grand families because her mother was a sister of the Marquess of Langsworth, but Sacha knew it was the other people who had counted to her mother and who mourned her because she had left a gap in their lives which nobody else could fill.

She knew that her aunt, the present Marchioness, would never be mourned in the same way, and although she did not wish to think of it, she could not help feeling that if Deirdre became the Duchess of Silchester she would be kind and friendly only to those who were her social equals, and would have little or no concern for the unimportant people who lived on the Duke's vast estates.

Her father had always said the most important thing people could give was themselves.

Sacha thought that was what she would like to have the opportunity of doing if she married a man who had many people dependent upon him, then when she died there would be genuine mourners at her Funeral, as there had been at her mother's.

But she told herself laughingly that this was not the moment to be thinking about death.

For the first time in her quiet life she was living fully, even if somewhat reprehensibly.

'In fact,' she thought, 'I am seeing the world outside Little Langsworth, as I never expected to do.'

The Hall was not far from London, and as the train was a fast one and only stopped at three stations, they reached Paddington just before eleven o'clock.

For a moment the crowded platform with the porters jostling to get to the carriage doors and the noise from the engines standing at the platforms made Sacha feel panic-stricken.

Then a Guard came to unlock the door and behind him there was a thin, studious-looking man wearing spectacles whom she was sure was Mr. Evans.

"Good morning, Your Ladyship!" he said. "The train is right on time, which is unusual."

"Thank you for meeting me," Sacha replied, holding out her hand.

As Mr. Evans seemed rather surprised she thought perhaps she should have been more formal with him.

A porter collected her hand-baggage which included the luxurious fitted dressing-case which Deirdre had given her.

"You cannot give me that!" Sacha had exclaimed when she saw it. "Let me just borrow it, and I will return it to you afterwards."

"I have no further use for it," Deirdre replied loftily. "The brushes are all fitted in silver, but now I have one in gold which Papa gave me last Christmas. I was going to throw it away, so you might as well make use of it."

"Thank you . . . very much."

Sacha could not help thinking that what the Marquess must have spent on the gold-fitted dressing-case for Deirdre would have kept them at the Vicarage in luxury for a whole year.

Then she told herself it was ridiculous to make comparisons, and she must just be overwhelmingly grateful that Deirdre like a Fairy Godmother had waved a magic wand and she was to have things she had never anticipated owning in her wildest dreams.

That was certainly true when it came to handbags and all the accessories which went with the gowns, including long suede gloves and such a profusion of shoes and slippers that Sacha was sure it would take her a lifetime to wear them out.

"I have two carriages waiting for you, My Lady," Mr. Evans was saying as Sacha stepped out of the train onto the platform. "I thought you and your lady's-maid could travel in one, and I will follow with the luggage."

"Thank you, that is very kind."

The carriages were very luxurious, and emblazoned with her Uncle's crest.

Sacha felt nervous in case the coachman or the footman on the box who obviously must know Deirdre would think she looked different from their young mistress, but they merely touched their cockaded top hats respectfully and Sacha was certain as she stepped into the carriage that they never gave her a second look.

They had to drive right across London to Kings Cross to catch the Scottish Express which was leaving at half after noon, and she felt as she drove through the crowded streets that Lord Gerard had been very clever to find two trains that connected so conveniently.

Kings Cross seemed a turmoil of trains, people, mountains of luggage, guards blowing whistles, while waving red flags, engines letting off steam and belching clouds of black smoke into the air.

Mr. Evans had reserved a First Class carriage for them and informed Sacha that he had made arrangements for hampers of food to be brought to them at every station and there was one already in their carriage which contained their luncheon.

Because they were to stay in the train all night, they were also provided with rugs and soft pillows, and Mr.

Evans gave Sacha a list of the stations at which the train stopped, so that Emily and she could if they wished, get out and walk on the platform.

He had punctiliously written in the length of time the train stayed at each station and Sacha though that nobody could have seen to their comfort more competently.

Mr. Evans then disappeared to purchase newspapers and a big pile of magazines.

"That is very kind of you," Sacha said, "but it seems somewhat extravagant."

She thought Mr. Evans looked surprised, then realising she was speaking as herself rather than as Deirdre she added quickly:

"I had forgotten how long the journey takes, so of course there will be plenty of time to read them all."

Then a sudden idea came to her and she said:

"I wonder, Mr. Evans, if you would be very kind and buy the sporting papers? I want to see which horses have been winning at Epsom."

A knowing look crossed Mr. Evans' face, and she was sure that like everybody else at the Hall, he was aware that Deirdre would soon be engaged to the Duke of Silchester.

Without saying anything he hurried back to the Book-stall and came back with three sporting papers which Sacha had very occasionally seen in her father's Study.

She thanked him, and once again shook him by the hand. Then the door of the compartment was locked, and the train moved off.

Mr. Evans stood back and bowed, and Sacha waved her hand which again she thought Deirdre would not have done, but which she was sure pleased him.

Then they were off on the long journey which would end up in Scotland.

It was in fact, a very, very long journey, but at the same time, Sacha enjoyed it.

The hampers which were brought to them at all the big stations made every meal seem like a picnic and although she did not eat very much Emily did full justice to everything that was provided.

They got out at Crewe because Sacha was interested in seeing the station, although she was aware that Emily was agitated all the time in case the train should go without them.

When night came Sacha arranged the pillows on the seats, and taking off her elegant bonnet placed it very carefully in the rack before she lay down and covered herself with a rug.

It was rather difficult because her crinoline was so big that it stuck up in the air. But there was nobody to see her pretty lace-trimmed petticoats underneath except for Emily who at first was rather nervous of lying down.

"I think I'd better sit up, Miss, in case we run into any trouble," she said.

"If we do, how will you prevent it by sitting up? Do not be silly, Emily, take the opportunity of sleeping while you can, and you will be much more comfortable without your shawl and bonnet."

Emily was finally persuaded to do as Sacha suggested, and when she had once accepted that the train would not run off the rails, she fell asleep while it was Sacha who lay awake thinking of what lay ahead.

* * *

When at about twelve o'clock noon the following day they passed over the Scottish border, Sacha thought it was a marvellous moment.

"I have always wanted to visit Scotland, Emily," she

said. "Think of it, we are now in the land of the moors and the heather, the land where Gentlemen shoot grouse, not pheasants, and the rivers are full of salmon."

"It looks a bit lonely, Miss," Emily said, staring out of the window, but Sacha was not listening.

"This is the land which has produced great Statesmen, explorers and pioneers, who have travelled all over the world," she said, "and of course, there was Robert the Bruce, Wallace and Bonny Prince Charlie."

She was speaking aloud to herself as she knew that Emily would not understand.

She felt it was all very romantic and she only wished they were coming to Scotland later in the year when the heather would be purple and she would, she thought, see the grouse swooping down over the moors into the glens.

Even so, the landscape was enchanting with its lochs forests and high hills. In fact, Scotland was just as she had expected it to be.

The timetable which Mr. Evans had compiled so painstakingly showed Sacha that they would arrive at the Halt for Strathconna Castle at three o'clock in the afternoon.

By this time however the train was running late. It was well after four o'clock when they finally drew up at the Halt and Sacha saw there were several people standing on a small platform, one of them wearing a kilt.

"We are being met by a man in a kilt!" she told Emily excitedly, but the maid was pulling on her black cotton gloves and only replied:

"It's strange, Miss, to think of a man wearing petticoats!"

Sacha gave a little laugh.

Then the door was opened and she was being helped out by the man in the kilt who also had a red beard, and there was another man wearing a bowler hat who was obviously a senior servant.

She was welcomed to Scotland, then escorted to where two carriages each drawn by four horses were waiting outside on the roadway.

This time, Sacha found, she was expected to travel alone in the first carriage while Emily went with the two servants and the baggage in the other.

The horses set off at a good pace and she leant forward to see the countryside. There were clumps of dark fir trees, and silver burns running through the moorland.

"It is very lovely!" she told herself and thought she must remember everything she saw so as to tell her father.

It was nearly an hour before she had her first glimpse of Strathconna Castle, silhouetted against the sky.

It was exactly, she thought, what a Scottish Castle should look like, high up the side of a hill, with below it a wide twisting river which she was sure would be filled with salmon.

It struck her that must be the reason why the Duke came North at this time of the year, as there would be nothing to shoot until the autumn.

Then she reasoned it out that as the grouse would be breeding, the gun-trap which had injured him would have been set for the wild-cats which were known to devour as many as twenty-five grouse a day, and were a menace on every moor.

'At the same time the traps are very cruel,' she thought, 'and the Duke's accident should dissuade the people in this vicinity, at any rate, from ever using them again.'

They reached the Castle, and because it was so beautiful, sheltered at the back by green fir trees with a standard flying from the top of the highest tower, Sacha forgot for the moment what was waiting for her there.

Then as the horses drove through gates which were flanked on each side by lodges fashioned like miniature castles, and down a long straight drive, she began to feel afraid.

Supposing the Duke knew at once that she was not the girl to whom he was engaged? Supposing he denounced her, and she was sent home ignominiously on the next train?

She would have to get in touch with Deirdre and tell her what had happened, and she could imagine only too well how angry her cousin would be and how she would despise her for being so stupid as to be discovered.

"Please, God, do not let him guess that I am not Deirdre," Sacha prayed in her heart.

Then hardly before the words were formed in her mind the carriage came to a standstill.

There was an enormous brass-studded front door, and waiting on the steps in front of it were two servants wearing kilts of the same tartan as that worn by the one who had met her.

The door of the carriage was opened, and feeling that her heart was turning somersaults in her breast and there were a dozen butterflies fluttering inside her, Sacha stepped down.

"Welcome to Strathconna Castle, M'Lady!" the servant in the kilt said with a broad Scots accent.

"Thank you," Sacha said shyly. "I am very glad to be here."

The servant, who she imagined was a Butler, went ahead of her, and having passed through a large Hall where there were many mounted heads of stags she climbed a broad staircase which led to the first floor.

Vaguely Sacha remembered either her mother or her father telling her that in Scottish Castles the main rooms were always on the first floor, although she could not now remember the reason for it.

When they reached the broad landing the high double doors in front of them were thrown open by a kilted servant who announced:

"Lady Deirdre Lang, Your Grace!"

For a moment Sacha was so frightened that she could see nothing but the afternoon sunshine coming in through three large windows.

Then she could see that at the far end of the room there was an elderly woman with white hair who was just rising from the chair in which she had been sitting.

She walked towards her and saw that the Dowager Duchess looked very old, and at the same time that when she was young she must have been beautiful.

Now her face appeared to Sacha soft and gentle, and reminded her in some way of her mother.

"How nice of you to come, my dear," the Duchess said as Sacha reached her and curtsied. "I am so delighted to meet you, and I know how thrilled Talbot will be that you are here."

"It is very kind of you to ask me," Sacha said. "How is . . . His Grace?"

She knew this was the first thing she should ask, but was not quite certain how she should refer to the Duke as they were not yet officially engaged.

"I have a lot to tell you about him," the Dowager Duchess replied, "but I know that you would first like to wash and have your tea, and I expect, change your gown."

She gave a little laugh.

"I know how stuffy one feels after that long train journey, which I find more exhausting every time I go South."

"I found it very interesting and exciting," Sacha said, "because I have never before been to the North of England, let alone to Scotland."

As she spoke she hoped she was not making a mistake and Deirdre had in fact done both, but she was sure if she had been as far as Scotland the news of it would somehow have percolated through to the village.

"Then it is certainly an experience you will repeat," the Duchess replied, "because Talbot comes to me every year for the salmon fishing."

Sacha was pleased to know she had been right in guessing that was the reason for the Duke's visit.

The Duchess led her from the room and down a long passage, where the floor was covered with tartan instead of ordinary carpet, to a bedroom that was on the same floor as the Drawing-Room.

It had besides a large four-poster bed, an open fireplace in which to her surprise, there was a log of wood smouldering.

Sacha saw the Duchess looking at it, and then she explained:

"Everybody who comes as far North as this is afraid of feeling cold, so I ordered a fire to be lit in your bedroom, my dear."

"That was very kind of you," Sacha exclaimed, "and what a lovely room!"

As she spoke she looked out of the window and realised that the view which was the same as from the Drawing-Room was of the moors stretching away into the distant horizon, and that in front of the Castle there was a large loch.

"You are looking at Loch Conna," the Duchess said, "and while you are here I must tell you of the legends about it which I am sure you will find very interesting."

"I am sure I will," Sacha agreed.

"And here is Mrs. Macdonald," the Duchess went on, "who is my Housekeeper and will look after you. By the time we have finished tea your luggage will have been brought upstairs and you will be able to change into a fresh gown before you visit Talbot."

*   *   *

A quarter of an hour later, Sacha was sampling with delight her first Scottish tea.

It was so exactly as she had expected it to be from what she had read in the books about Scotland that she longed for her father to be there so that they could laugh together at what she thought was enough food for a Regiment of soldiers.

There were scones, griddle-cakes, baps, shortbread and oatmeal biscuits.

There was honey which was made in the autumn from the heather blossom and was much darker than any honey she had seen before.

There was a special ginger cake which the Duchess said her grandson liked to take with him with his sandwiches for luncheon when he went fishing.

"If I am to eat all this," Sacha said, "I will be very fat by the time I leave the Castle!"

The Duchess laughed.

"We pride ourselves in the North on having better food than anywhere else in the British Isles and certainly the meals are very substantial."

"I believe Your Grace must be Scottish," Sacha said thinking as she asked the question that it was something she should have learned from Deirdre.

"Of course I am," the Duchess replied. "I was born a Macdonald, and when my husband, the second Duke, died I knew I would be happier in my own land with my own people than living amongst a lot of Sassenachs!"

She spoke the last words somewhat mockingly which made Sacha laugh.

"And you live here alone all the year?" she enquired.

"I have a lot of relations and friends living near me," the Duchess replied, "and in Scotland nobody makes a fuss about long journeys as they do in England."

She smiled before she explained:

"Guests think nothing of driving five or ten miles to a dinner-party and it is very usual to sleep where you eat."

"It sounds very pleasant and good-neighbourly."

"That is exactly what it is," the Duchess answered. "Now if you have finished, I think you should change your gown, then come and see Talbot, who I am sure is longing to thank you for coming such a long way."

As the Duchess did not rise from her place at the tea-table Sacha waited, feeling she had something important to add.

"I wanted you to come," the Duchess began, "because Talbot has been so depressed and worried about his eyes and I knew you would cheer him up."

"What can I do to . . . help?"

The Duchess paused before she said:

"The Doctors are very optimistic, but they have insisted on his keeping his eyes bandaged until they are quite certain there is no danger of the light affecting them, as sometimes happens after an accident."

"You do not . . . think the Duke will be . . . permanently

blind?" Sacha asked anxiously.

"I know that is what is worrying him," the Duchess answered, "and I want you to persuade him to trust the doctors and his good luck, which is proverbial on the race-course as everywhere else."

The Duchess gave a little sigh before she continued:

"It was certainly bad luck that he should have walked into a gun-trap which had been set in a place where fisherman seldom go, and was some way from the river."

"I think gun-traps are horrible and cruel!" Sacha said impulsively without thinking that it might be rude to express her personal opinion so strongly.

"I am now convinced you are right," the Duchess agreed, "and I have told the gamekeepers they are not to be used any longer on my estate."

"I am very glad about that," Sacha said, "but how badly was His Grace hurt otherwise?"

"He had to have quite a number of pieces of metal removed from his body," the Duchess replied, "but the doctors were delighted that he is so strong that the wounds have healed quickly and without becoming in any way infected."

She paused before she continued:

"But he has to have another operation to remove a further piece of metal and because it has been a shock they are very anxious that he should be kept as quiet as possible, and this is essential where it concerns his eyes."

"I understand," Sacha said.

"What you have to do my dear, is to persuade him to do what the doctors think is best, and not, in the words of St. Paul, to 'kick against the pricks.'"

"I will try," Sacha said simply.

The Duchess rose.

"Now hurry to your room and change, and I will be waiting for you in the Drawing-Room."

As there seemed to be some urgency in the Duchess's voice Sacha ran down the passage and found when she reached her bedroom that Emily was there and with the help of Mrs. Macdonald and two other young house-maids was unpacking the trunks she had brought with her.

She had seen only a very brief glimpse of the clothes which Deirdre had given her because Hannah had already partially packed one case, and they had been too con-cerned in discussing what she should wear for the journey to show her what was to go into the other trunk.

Now she saw that the wardrobe was filled with gowns of every colour and made with a great variety of mate-rials.

She felt her spirits lift and thought that nothing could be more thrilling than for the first time in her life to be dressed in gowns which came from Bond Street.

They would, because she had the same colour hair and eyes as Deirdre, make her feel she was part of this fairy-tale Castle in a land that was as lovely and exciting as the legends had described which she had read when she was a child.

There was however, no time now to look through what she had brought with her, and Mrs. Macdonald lifted from the wardrobe a very attractive leaf-green gown that had a crinoline decorated with bows of green velvet ribbon.

Real lace edged the sleeves and the neck, and there were little green velvet slippers to peep beneath the hem of the crinoline, and a bow to wear in her hair at the back of her head.

Emily tidied her hair which was arranged in the same

style as Deirdre's, and when Sacha looked at herself in the mirror she could not help feeling that she herself had vanished, and the reflection she saw was actually that of her cousin.

Then she remembered that the Duchess was waiting, and hurried to the Drawing-Room.

"You have been very quick, my dear!" the Duchess exclaimed, "and you look lovely! Talbot told me that you were the most beautiful girl he had ever seen, and I know now he was not exaggerating!"

"That is very kind of Your Grace," Sacha replied shyly.

"I am only so sad," the Duchess said, "that he cannot see you in that beautiful gown, but I know it is only a question of time before he will be himself again."

By now they were walking down the corridor and she gave Sacha a little smile as she added:

"Of course as I am Scottish I believe I am clairvoyant, and therefore when I say Talbot will be himself again, I am prophesying what will come true."

"I very much hope so," Sacha said.

Because she knew that in a moment she was going to see the Duke, her fears that he might denounce her as an imposter had all returned. The butterflies were fluttering inside her, and she felt as if her voice had died in her throat.

They had nearly reached the end of the passage when they came to a high impressive-looking door. It was opened immediately by a small wiry-looking little man who said respectfully:

"'Afternoon, Y'Grace! 'Afternoon, M'Lady!"

"How is your patient, Tomkins?" the Duchess asked.

"I think His Grace's better."

The Duchess turned to Sacha.

"Tomkins has been with my grandson ever since he grew up. He is a far better nurse than anyone the doctors can provide, and in many ways a much better doctor. Is that not true, Tomkins?"

"I be only too ready to agree with that, Y'Grace," Tomkins said with a grin.

The Duchess laughed.

They were standing inside what was a small Hall, and now Tomkins crossed it to open a door.

"It's 'Er Grace an' Lady Deirdre, Y'Grace!" he said with what seemed to Sacha almost a cockney accent.

Then as she held her breath they were in a large room and she could see a man lying in a huge carved four-poster bed with a bandage covering his eyes.

The Duchess walked towards him.

"Deirdre has arrived, Talbot," she said. "After a long and tiring journey from England. I cannot tell you how glad I am to meet her and know that you were telling me the truth when you said how beautiful she was."

"You are there, Deirdre?"

The Duke's voice was low and very deep.

After a second, because she was frightened, Sacha moved forward to stand nearer to the bed before she answered him in a voice that did not sound like her own:

"Yes...I am...here!"

"It was good of you to come."

The Duke put out his hand as he spoke and because she knew it was expected, Sacha put her fingers into it.

She knew as she touched him that she was trembling and hoped he would not be aware of it, and then as his fingers closed over hers, he said:

"You are cold!"

"I have given her a fire in her bedroom," the Duchess said quickly.

Sacha tried to think of something to say, but she was only conscious of the strength of his fingers and felt there was a power flowing from his touch.

She could not explain it to herself, and yet it was undoubtedly there, something she felt which made him different from other people, and which seemed to vibrate from his hand to hers.

As if she knew she was embarrassed the Duchess said:

"I am going to leave you two young people, and I am sure you have a lot to say to each other. I do not think, Deirdre dear, you should stay very long because you are Talbot's first visitor, except for me, and you too must be tired and should lie down before dinner."

Without waiting for an answer she went from the room, and as the door closed behind her Sacha was aware that the Duke was still holding her hand.

"I am surprised to see you!" he said.

"Surprised?"

"I did not think you would come, although my grandmother told me she had written to ask you to do so."

"I . . . I was so very . . . sorry to hear of your . . . accident."

"Did it really worry you?" the Duke asked.

"But, of course!" Sacha replied. "It was . . . terrible for you, and your grandmother has ordered that there shall be no more gun-traps on her land. Papa has always . . . denounced them as diabolical . . ."

As she spoke she realised she was speaking as herself and not as Deirdre, and hoped that the Duke would not suspect that her Uncle would be only too willing to use any means to prevent his precious pheasants from being disturbed or poached.

The Duke released her hand and Sacha looked round to find there was a chair just behind her, and sat down.

Now she could look at him without being so agitated

she saw in fact that he was an extremely handsome man.

He had a broad forehead from which his dark hair was brushed back, a straight, aristocratic nose, a square chin, and a very firm and decisive mouth.

She had the feeling that if his eyes were not bandaged he would be formidable and very frightening, but because he was lying back against his pillows he was not as terrifying as she had anticipated he would be.

"What Balls and parties did you have to give up to come to see me?" the Duke asked, and she thought there was a slightly mocking note in his voice.

"They . . . did not concern me . . . because I was . . . worried about you," Sacha said.

"I am honoured and of course flattered," the Duke replied, "but quite frankly, I would have bet one-hundred to one against your not finding some excuse for not coming to Scotland. I know how much you really dislike the country!"

"How could anybody dislike anything so beautiful as this Castle?"

Then almost as if she was speaking to herself Sacha said:

"When I was coming here I felt as if I had stepped into the past. I could see the Scotsmen gathering in the glens and creeping out at night to raid another Clan, and take from them their sheep and their cattle."

The Duke did not speak and she went on:

"I thought too of them hiding when the Vikings came across the North Sea and pillaged the villagers and of course who could be in Scotland and not think of Bonny Prince Charlie, and the loyalty and love he evoked in a crusade which ended so disastrously?"

There was a little throb in Sacha's voice because the tragedy of the Young Pretender had always moved her very deeply.

Then feeling she had said too much she was silent, and after a moment the Duke said:

"You surprise me, Deirdre, because I had no idea you would feel like that! It is what I actually feel myself, when I am in Scotland!"

"Do you think about the past when you are fishing?"

"Sometimes," he replied, "but usually I am watching for a salmon and making surè I strike at exactly the right moment!"

"It must be fascinating!"

"Are you telling me that you would like to learn to fish?"

"I would love to do so!" Sacha said eagerly.

Then she remembered it was something that would never happen, and when the Duke was well enough to fish again she would be back in the Vicarage, and he would be with Deirdre.

"That certainly inspires me to get better as quickly as possible," he said.

"You know it is something you have to do," Sacha answered. "If one is determined enough in life one always gets what one wants."

"Is that your philosophy?"

Sacha thought for a moment, then she said:

"My sort of will-power, which is concentration, meditation and of course what the Church has for two thousand years called prayer is, I think, always answered, if the cause is . . . right."

She spoke in the same way that she would have spoken to her father, and while it was impossible to see the expression on the Duke's face because of his bandages, she thought he was surprised.

Then he asked:

"Are you telling me that you have been praying for me, Deirdre?"

"Of course I have!" Sacha answered.

As she spoke she remembered that if she was honest she should add that she had also been praying that he would accept her for who she was pretending to be, and would not be suspicious that she was somebody else.

chapter three

SACHA awoke and for the moment could not think where she was.

The sun coming from between the curtains revealed the huge, high-ceilinged room, the open fireplace in which a log had burnt itself out, and the carved posts of the bed.

She was in Scotland!

Then everything came back to her, and she remembered leaving the Duke, walking down the passage to her own bedroom, and finding Emily waiting for her, then saying:

"Your bath's not ready yet, M'Lady. Why don't you get into bed and have a rest? You can have half an hour, and I'm sure you're tired."

"That is true," Sacha agreed.

Because there seemed to be no point in refusing, she let Emily help her into a nightgown and slipped between the sheets in the big bed.

Almost as soon as her head touched the pillow she fell asleep and she realised now that she had not been wakened for dinner, but had slept right through the night.

She knew that she had been so tired, not only because she had had very little sleep on the train, but also because she had been so afraid that the Duke might know she was an imposter, and had therefore been tense and on edge, as well as frightened.

She had however passed her first test with flying colours, and she had dropped into a dreamless sleep which made her feel now as if she was awakening to a whole new world.

She sat up in bed, and her first impulse was to jump out and draw back the curtains. Then she knew that Deirdre would ring for Hannah, and not think of moving until everything was arranged for her.

She was sure that Emily would be some time because the Castle was so big, but it was in fact only very few minutes before she came bustling into her room.

"You're awake, M'Lady!" she said. "You've had a real good night."

"I am afraid I missed dining with the Duchess, and that seems very rude," Sacha replied.

Emily walked across the room to pull back the curtains. As she did so she chatted.

"Last night, M'Lady, Mrs. Macdonald came along to see if everything was all right, and when she saw you were fast asleep she went and asked Her Grace if we should wake you."

"I presume she said 'no.'"

"Her Grace said: 'Let her sleep. She deserves it coming all this way!'"

Sacha laughed.

"Everybody talks as if I have flown to the moon, or dived down to the bottom of the sea. After all, although it took a long time, it was a very comfortable journey."

"T'was not as frightening as I thought it were goin' to be," Emily conceded, "but if Your Ladyship asks me, I don't like trains!"

Sacha had no answer to this, so she only laughed.

Emily brought her some hot water, and after she had washed she chose one of the plainest gowns which Deirdre had given her, thinking that in Scotland it would be a mistake to be overdressed.

It was however very becoming, and although she felt slightly flamboyant in her large crinoline she knew as she walked along the corridor to find the Duchess that she looked very elegant, and not in the least like the old-fashioned, threadbare figure she appeared at the Vicarage.

Because she was thinking of her clothes, she did not realise that her eyes were alight with interest and seemed to have caught the sunshine, and that every movement she made had a grace that made the Duchess think of the young deer that were roaming the moors outside.

"Please forgive me, Your Grace, for being so rude," Sacha pleaded. "I lay down for a little while last night, and knew nothing until I awoke about half an hour ago."

"I think it was a very sensible thing to do," the Duchess replied, "and now I am sure you want to see my grandson before I take you round the Castle or, as it is such a lovely day, we might explore the garden first."

"I want to see everything!" Sacha agreed. "I am quite

certain that I have walked into a fairy-story!"

"And of course, as you are going to be married to 'Prince Charming,' that is the happy ending we all seek," the Duchess smiled.

Her words made Sacha remember that her fairy-story would end abruptly with her return to the Vicarage, and she was intelligent enough to know that because it would be dangerous Deirdre would never allow her to see the Duke again.

That meant that when there were parties at the Hall she would not be invited, and she rather doubted if she would receive an invitation to the wedding.

Then she thought philosophically that she might as well enjoy herself while she could, and if she was Cinderella, at least her Fairy Godmother had provided her with beautiful gowns, a train instead of a glass coach, and she must remember when she went, not to leave one of her glass slippers behind.

Not, she told herself with a smile, that the Duke would be likely to seek for her, and when she left the Castle she must never think of him.

They reached the Duke's apartment, and Tomkins opened the door.

"How is His Grace this morning?" the Duchess asked.

Tomkins lowered his voice.

"His Grace had a bad night, Yer Grace! I'm afraid 'e's in one of 'is dark moods."

"Oh, dear!" the Duchess said. "In that case I think it would be best if Her Ladyship saw him alone. She is far more likely to lift his spirits than I am."

She put her hand on Sacha's arm and said:

"Cheer him up, dear. It is such a mistake for him to feel despondent when he needs all his strength for the next operation, and of course for his eyes."

She did not wait for Sacha to reply, but walked back the way they had come and Tomkins waited a moment before he opened the door into the Duke's bedroom.

"Here's 'er Ladyship to see you, Your Grace."

Feeling rather nervous Sacha walked towards the bed.

She thought the Duke was lying lower on his pillows than he had the day before, and when she could see his face clearly she saw his mouth was set as if in a tight line.

She was sure that if she could see his eyes they would be stormy with a frown between them.

"It is a lovely day," she said, "which I feel is a special welcome to Scotland for me. Do you want me to describe what the view looks like?"

There was a pause as if the Duke was surprised at what she had said.

Then he replied in a disagreeable tone:

"You may as well tell me what you see, for as I am blind and likely to remain so, there is nothing I can do but listen."

Sacha walked to one of the windows and looked out.

"It is so lovely," she said, "that there are no words in which to describe the different lights on the moors, the reflection of the sky on the loch, and everything is bathed in sunshine that seems more brilliant than the sun in the South."

"Very poetical!" the Duke remarked and she knew he was being sarcastic. "As I may have to rely on your description of what is around me for the rest of my life, I am glad you have such a command of the English language!"

Sacha walked back to the bed.

"Are you really being so foolish as to think you may not regain your sight?" she enquired.

"I do not want to talk about it," the Duke snapped. "It is bad enough lying here blind and useless without putting it into words."

"Is that what you are really thinking about yourself?" Sacha asked. "Because if so, it is the most stupid thing you could do!"

"What do you mean by that?"

"Surely you must be aware," she replied, "that what we think we become? Not only mentally, but physically."

"That is sheer nonsense!"

"But," Sacha argued, "you must have read books and heard stories of people who were healed unexpectedly because they believed."

"Are you talking about miracles?" the Duke asked.

"Miracles are the more spectacular examples of healing which are accepted by the Church, and therefore recorded in books so that we can read about them. But everyday small miracles occur which slip by without anybody noticing them, but nevertheless are examples of thinking the right thoughts, or, if you prefer to do so, call it faith."

There was a long pause and she knew the Duke was thinking over what she had said. Then he replied almost aggressively as if he wished to argue with her:

"I cannot believe there is any medical substantiation for what you are saying, and the fanatics of every religion get carried away into believing they can be helped by the supernatural when they are too weak or effete to help themselves."

"Religious faith can be very spectacular, and has amazing results," Sacha replied. "One has only to think of Mecca, of the Holy Men in India, or the long list of Catholic Saints who according to the Church performed innumerable miracles."

She paused, and as the Duke did not speak she went on quickly:

"I am talking about little people who can think themselves well because they believe with their hearts and minds that they will recover and so they do."

"Have you really come in contact with such people?" the Duke asked.

There was a cynical note in his voice which told Sacha he thought she was just making up what she was saying to impress him.

Sacha thought quickly, remember that as Deirdre she could not have had the contact that she had had herself, with poor people.

Then because she wished to go on arguing with the Duke, and was sure that what she was saying was important, she replied:

"My Uncle is the Vicar of Little Langsworth. He is a very good man, and he has often told me of the people he has helped back to health by making them believe it is possible!"

She thought this sounded very plausible, and went on:

"His wife, my Aunt Margaret, helped them by making them eat the right food, the right herbs, and other natural products, which swept away their illnesses and restored them to good health."

"What you are saying," the Duke said, "is that my thinking is wrong, and so is what I am eating."

Because he seemed to be mocking her, Sacha was silent for a moment. Then she said:

"You may think it rather . . . presumptuous of . . . me, but I know if I was in your place I would never allow . . . bad thoughts to retard the process of healing."

"I suppose by 'bad thoughts' you are referring to my fear that I may be permanently blind."

"I am positive there is no chance of that," Sacha answered. "At the same time, you may prolong the time that you have to wear a bandage, and retard the healing which should, because you are young and strong, be very quick."

"Do you really believe you know what you are talking about?" the Duke asked.

"It may sound conceited, but I do know, and it is logical and sensible if you think it out."

"Very well," the Duke conceded, "I will listen to your contentions if you put them a little more clearly. But I am not going to accept what you tell me is anything but a fantasy without any medical research to back it."

Sacha laughed.

"My Aunt always said that people treat Doctors as if they had divine powers, when actually they are just ordinary men playing about with medicines they have not tried themselves, and which half the time they do not understand."

"That is certainly very scathing."

"I am . . . sorry," Sacha said quickly. "I do not wish to undermine your confidence in your Doctors. I just want you to realise that if you apply your mind to it you can heal yourself."

"I am prepared to listen to your extraordinary ideas on the subject," the Duke said, "so tell me quite simply what you expect me to do."

Sacha was watching the movement of his lips and she knew just as if she had been able to see the expression in his eyes that he was sceptical of everything she was saying, and also thinking it was impertinent of her to lecture him.

She rose from the chair in which she had been sitting by his bedside.

"I am going to get something which I would like to read to you, and perhaps it will make you understand what I am trying to say."

She did not wait for him to agree, but ran from the room along the passage and back to her own bedroom.

She had brought with her, because she had thought it would support her and give her courage, two of her father's books.

She always kept them by her bedside, and usually read little bits of them at night, after she had said her prayers.

She picked up one now, and went back to the Duke's bedroom shutting the outside door, then the bedroom one behind her.

He did not speak, and she sat down again beside him. She had the feeling that he had been waiting for her and was at least interested in what she had to say.

Because she was at the moment breathless from running down the passage, she turned over the pages slowly, until she found what she wanted. Then she said:

"I know that at the moment you will not agree with me when I tell you that if you think only of the misery of being blind, you will slow down the healing of your eyes. Instead I want you to think of the light—the light which to the Greeks was life itself."

The Duke did not speak, and picking up her book she read slowly and softly:

"At dawn the whole body of Apollo poured across the sky, intensely virile, flashing with a million points of light, healing everything it touched, germinating the seeds and defying the powers of darkness."

She paused, wondering if the Duke would say anything.

He was lying very still, and yet she knew instinctively that he was listening. So she went on:

"He was not the sun only, he was the moon, the planets, the Milky Way, and the faintest stars: he was the sparkle of the waves, the gleam in eyes, and the shining of a girl's face. He was the strange glimmer of fields on the darkest nights, and whenever a spring issued from a mountain, he was present at the moment when it emerged into the light."

She put the book down on her knees and said:

"Light heals! That is the light I want you to think about: the light which is holy and life itself."

The Duke still did not speak, and because she suddenly felt embarrassed and thought she should not have spoken to him so positively, she rose to her feet to walk back to the window.

She looked out again at the light varying from purple to gold on the moors, the glimmer of sunshine on the rocks, the blue of the sky, and felt only the Greeks could have put into words what she was seeing.

Then from the bed she heard a voice say:

"Where are you, Deirdre? I want to talk to you!"

"I am here," Sacha said, quickly moving back towards him. "I went to the window because I was afraid perhaps you were... angry at what I said to you."

"I am not in the least angry," the Duke replied, "only surprised. I had no idea you knew about such things, and they are certainly new to me."

"But you must have studied Greek when you were at the University?"

"That was a long time ago."

"If once one has read about the Greeks," Sacha said, "I do not think one would ever forget."

As if it was a train of thought he did not wish to follow, the Duke said, she thought evasively:

"I will certainly think about what you have just told me, and that of course covers the mind."

"My cure also involves eating the right foods."

"I hardly think my grandmother would be very pleased to hear that!"

"I am sure the food here is excellent for you ordinarily," Sacha said. "What could be better for you than fresh salmon from the river and grouse from the moors?"

"Not at this time of the year."

"I know that," Sacha answered, "and when I was coming North I was wishing I could see the heather in bloom and even more beautiful than it is at the moment."

"That is easy," the Duke said. "We will return here in August."

Sacha felt a little pang of regret because while he might be able to return, it was something she would never do. It was very unlikely she would ever see the moors glowing purple and the grouse winging down the glens.

"I am waiting," the Duke said. "What are you thinking about?"

"I was thinking how lovely everything would look in August, and yet finding it hard to believe that it could be more beautiful than it is at this moment."

"I am concerned to hear what food you believe is magical enough to heal my body."

Once again Sacha knew that he was being sarcastic, and while she half wished she had not started this conversation in the first place, she somehow felt compelled to tell him what she believed.

She knew in her heart of hearts it would help him,

just as her mother had helped so many people in the past, and she would have thought it wrong to leave anybody in ignorance of what would really do them good.

"I expect," she began, "that since in Scotland the season is later than in England for vegetables and fruit, you will find in the garden here all the things which heal as well as nourish."

"What are they?"

"First for your eyes," she said, "you should have fresh young carrots, and as many green vegetables as possible. I am sure there will be peas, cabbages, spinach and all sorts of other things available."

"I expect I am eating those already."

"But not, I suspect, in very large amounts, uncooked."

Sacha hesitated. Then she added:

"I would like to suggest, if you do not think your grandmother would be offended, that the cook should prepare carrot juice for you, you should have salads with every meal, and perhaps one dish of nothing but young green vegetables."

The Duke laughed.

"Are you really suggesting that this everyday food is better than the pills, tablets and potions with which the Doctors have provided me?"

"I am not going to compare them," Sacha said in a low voice, "but the vegetables are provided by God, and are therefore pure and filled with the goodness that comes from the soil, and not from a factory."

"How can you know all this?" the Duke asked unexpectedly. "Have you been reading some fashionable book, or have you just made it up to sweep away my depression about myself?"

"At the moment, since you are unable to look at a person to see if they are telling the truth or a lie," Sacha said, "you have to use your instinct, and that is something we all of us neglect."

"Are you saying my instinct should be so acute that I can judge people's character and everything else about them without references and without being able to tell by seeing them whether they are deceiving me or not?"

"Of course I mean that! You should be able to know by the tone of their voices and, more important, by what you feel when they are near you."

"I can think of a better way than that."

As he spoke the Duke put out his hand saying:

"Let me touch you. I have the idea it will be the equivalent of looking at you. I shall then know if you are telling the truth or lying."

For a moment Sacha hesitated. She was almost afraid of his touching her in case his instinct told him she was not who she pretended to be.

She felt she should never have got involved in this sort of conversation since she realised now it was very unlike anything Deirdre would have said.

She certainly would not know about the Greeks or about healing people or eating the right food.

'I have been very silly,' Sacha thought with a kind of panic.

Yet she knew that since she wanted to help the Duke she had been compelled to tell him what he should do; for she knew it was the right advice, and was what her mother would have done in the same circumstances.

Then because he was waiting, and his hand lay open and turned upward on the sheet in front of him, she rather tentatively and nervously put her fingers on to his palm.

As she did so she felt exactly as she had the day before, when a vibration almost like a little shaft of light had moved from his hand to hers.

"It is," she told herself, "because he is so strong and such an overwhelming personality."

At the same time it made her rather afraid, and she thought that once again her fingers were trembling.

"My instinct tells me I can believe you," the Duke said slowly.

"I am glad about that," Sacha replied. "I would have been very upset if you had thought I was . . . lying."

The Duke's fingers tightened on hers.

"I think it would be hard for you to lie," he said, "and it would be very obvious if you were doing so to anybody who knew you well or—loved you."

Sacha drew in her breath and the Duke asked:

"Have you ever been in love?"

"No . . . never!"

As she spoke she wondered if that was the right thing to say, or if she should have added: "except with you."

But because of what the Duke had said, she somehow felt obliged to tell the truth, and that if she said anything else he would have been aware of it.

Then as she felt she must make things a little better she said in a low voice:

"We are . . . of course . . . talking about the . . . past."

"Yes, of course," the Duke agreed. "I am glad you have never been in love, except of course, with me."

Now there was again that cynical note in his voice which made Sacha feel uncomfortable, and quickly to change the subject she took her hand from his, saying, as she did so:

"Will you give my ideas a try? Will you think of light? The light in which the Greeks believed, and which healed everything it touched? And will you, if I can persuade your grandmother's cook to prepare them for you, eat

66

and drink the vegetables that I know will heal your wounds?"

"If it will please you, I will certainly give your somewhat unorthodox ideas a trial," the Duke answered. "And of course, if I get well quite naturally and in a normal way you will take all the credit!"

"On the contrary, as I have just pointed out," Sacha said, "the credit will be yours."

She was arguing with him as she would have argued with her father when they tried to cap each other's contentions, which she had found fascinating and more enjoyable than anything else in her quiet life.

Now the Duke said, and he was not mocking her:

"What else did your study of the Greeks teach you?"

"I think anybody who has studied Greek knows that they taught the world, the modern world, to think. It was the Greeks who made men believe in themselves and it was Socrates who advanced the frontiers of thinking more than any single man has ever done before or since."

Sacha was once again talking as she would have done with her father, and only as she finished speaking did she realise instinctively that the Duke was surprised and at the same time a little bewildered.

'I am making a mistake,' she thought unhappily. 'Deirdre would never talk like this. If I go on, he will guess that I am not the girl to whom he is engaged, and that will be disastrous.'

With an effort she said lightly:

"We cannot continue to talk so seriously when I have something very exciting to tell you."

"What is that?"

"Your horse won the third race at Newmarket on Monday."

"How on earth do you know that?" the Duke asked. "I have not been informed of it!"

"I suppose the newspapers have not reached here yet, or else you have not asked for them to be read to you. It was in *The Sporting-News* which I read in the train yesterday."

The Duke did not reply and she added quickly:

"How foolish of me to have left it behind! I should have brought it with me."

"Now I think about it," the Duke said, "nobody has mentioned the newspapers to me since my accident. I suppose it is another way of keeping me quiet. Ring the bell, and I will order them to be brought to me immediately!"

He spoke in such a loud voice that Sacha said:

"If you speak like that your grandmother and, I am sure, Tomkins will be very angry with me for exciting you."

"I am not excited," the Duke snapped.

"Well, whatever you like to call it, you are not keeping quiet as the doctors ordered."

"I thought you were my doctor now. You have certainly assumed that position!"

Sacha laughed.

"Now you are frightening me. If you say very much more, I am quite certain your grandmother will send me back by the next train!"

The Duke smiled and she thought that if his eyes were not bandaged it would transform his face.

"That is something to be avoided at all costs," he said. "Shall I say that I am not only enjoying having you here, but am fascinated and intrigued as to how very different you are from what I expected?"

"I only...hope you will not be...disappointed," Sacha remarked.

"I had the idea, and I suppose it was foolish of me, that you were only interested in the gaieties of London—the Court Receptions, and especially the Balls in which you undoubtedly were the most beautiful girl present."

Sacha thought quickly what she should reply to this. Then she said lightly:

"As we can hardly have a Ball here in the Castle by ourselves, I think perhaps it would be a good idea for us to explore our other interests. Of course one of the most important is your horses."

"I thought you were not particularly keen on racing, except on appearing at Royal Ascot, and you certainly never bothered to ride in London."

"There were so many other things to do," Sacha said quickly, "and anyway, I heard you rode very early in the morning, before the Park grew too crowded."

This was a bold presumption but almost as if she was being prompted in her duel of words with the Duke, she remembered her mother had told her that when she was a girl it had always been fun to ride very early.

"All the young men rode in the Park, before breakfast," Lady Margaret had said, "because it was not so crowded."

"You seem to have an explanation for everything," the Duke remarked, "but I am intrigued by discovering new aspects of your character which I never knew existed."

He smiled before he added:

"You have certainly made me think, and that was your first lesson for your patient."

Sacha wrinkled her nose.

"I think that sounds very pedestrian for someone as distinguished as you," she said. "It would be better to think of you as a wounded warrior, or perhaps a Knight in shining armour who has been mauled by a dragon."

She laughed as she added:

"It is very easy to believe in dragons in the darkness of the fir forests, just as I would not be in the least surprised if there were nymphs or sirens living deep down in the loch."

"I must admit I have never seen one," the Duke replied, "but dragons are a different thing, or perhaps you prefer the ghosts and ghouls which abound in every Highland legend which concerns a Castle."

"If there is a legend about this Castle," Sacha said quickly, "I would love to read it."

"I think first you should read to me about my horse winning at Newmarket, and if I promise not to get excited, perhaps you would condescend to ring the bell."

"I will do anything you want," Sacha replied, "but, please, give my ideas a chance and remember that restlessness, tension, irritation and above all anger are all extremely bad for you, and must be avoided at all costs."

The Duke laughed.

"How could I have imagined for one moment," he said, "that the most beautiful girl I have ever seen would turn out to be a Witch, because that is what you undoubtedly are. In Scotland a century ago you would have been burned at the stake!"

"I have read of the cruelty that was practised in this country towards Witches," Sacha said, "but I do not want to think about it."

"Do you always brush everything unpleasant under the carpet?" the Duke asked. "It is not a very practical way of facing the world."

Sacha did not reply and he laughed again.

"I know exactly what you are thinking, and what you are going to say; that if you think bad thoughts, then bad things will happen to you. But surely the cruelty of the past cannot have an effect either on the mind or the body."

"I am not going to reply to that because you know what I would say," Sacha answered. "Do you really want me to ask for the newspapers?"

"I am not certain if you are running away from my arguments or if you have another reason for it."

She thought he was certainly more perceptive than she had given him credit for! Also he might be sensing that she was feeling frightened because everything she had said was so unlike Deirdre!

She thought she heard a movement outside the door and without saying any more she rose from her chair and opened it.

As she expected, Tomkins was there, holding a tray in his hand on which there was a jug, a cup and a saucer.

"I was just coming to ask you to fetch the newspapers for His Grace," Sacha said.

"Of course, M'Lady, and I've got some 'elevenses' for 'Is Grace to take now."

"What is it?" the Duke asked in an uncompromising voice.

"Just somethin' Cook thinks be nourishing, Yer Grace."

"If it is the same broth as I had yesterday you can throw it down the drain!" the Duke said.

"I have a better idea," Sacha interrupted. "Please, will you ask the cook to squeeze the juice of some carrots into a glass together with the juice of some fresh celery? Add a very little salt and pepper, then stir it together thoroughly."

"That sounds a strange sort o' drink," Tomkins remarked.

"His Grace is willing to try it, and I am sure it will do him good."

Tomkins looked towards the bed, and as if he guessed that was what he was doing, the Duke said:

"Go on, Tomkins! You have your orders!"

"Very good, Yer Grace," Tomkins said in a resigned tone.

He went from the room and Sacha gave a little laugh.

"Do you think the kitchen staff will walk out?" she asked. "I am sure in Scotland they hate innovations even more than they do at home."

"I am not concerned with their feelings, but with my own," the Duke replied. "I have a suspicion that everything that is 'good for me' will taste disgusting!"

"That is a very bigoted point of view!"

Then they were arguing again, arguing for the sheer enjoyment of it, and they were both quite surprised when Tomkins returned with the carrot juice in a glass.

"Cook says, M'Lady, she's been asked for some strange things in her time, but she's never met anybody yet who drinks vegetables!"

Sacha chuckled.

"I thought it would cause a revolution."

"I will try it," the Duke said, "but I do not promise to take more than a sip or two, if it tastes as I suspect it will."

Tomkins put the glass into his hand and the Duke raised it to his lips.

He took a very small sip, then as if it was not altogether unpalatable another, then another.

Only when he had drunk half the glass did he say:

"I must admit, it is not as unpleasant as I expected."

"I cannot think why you are not generous enough to admit that you like it," Sacha said.

"Very well then, I like it!" the Duke replied, and she clapped her hands with delight.

"Please Tomkins," she said. "See that His Grace has three glasses that size every day . . . one in the morning, one after luncheon, and one sometime during the evening."

"Very well, M'Lady," Tomkins said in a resigned voice, "but I'm sure downstairs they'll think that any man that doesn't drink whisky has got something 'awfa' wrong wi' 'im!"

He took the empty glass from the Duke and left the room.

As Sacha laughed the Duke joined in, and this time his laughter was unrestrained.

chapter four

SACHA took a long time choosing which evening-gown she would wear.

Every time she opened the wardrobe in her room and saw the profusion of lovely gowns which Deirdre had given her she felt they could not really be hers.

After years of wearing the plain cotton dresses which were all that Nanny was capable of making, and finding it hard to afford even new ribbons with which to decorate them, it seemed incredible that she should now be the owner of such glorious clothes that they might have stepped out of a fairy-story.

But that, she told herself, was exactly what they had done, because as she had thought when she arrived, the Castle, herself and the Duke were all part of a fantasy.

Sometimes she would lie awake at night and wonder

what she would feel when she went back to the Vicarage knowing that she must never see the Duke again.

What was more she must not talk, even to her father, about her time here.

Perhaps later, when the Duke and Deirdre were safely married, she would confide in him and tell him what had happened, but she knew he would be distressed by her deceit and perhaps it would be a mistake to worry him.

'He may have so many worries already,' Sacha thought with a little sigh.

At the moment however they seemed far away and she could only stare at the rainbow hues of her gowns, and wonder which would be the most becoming.

When she described to the Duke what she had been doing and the weather outside, he had taken to asking her what she was wearing.

She had no idea that there was a rapt little note in her voice when she described her appearance which both intrigued and puzzled him.

This evening before she had left him to change for dinner, he had said:

"I know Grandmama goes to bed early, so come and say goodnight to me. You can then tell me about your gown so that I may visualise it as you expect me to do."

Sacha laughed before she replied:

"Although you can use your intuition about most things, I think it would be difficult for you to guess the colour of my gown or the material of which it is made."

"Do not be too sure!" the Duke replied. "Under your tuition, Madam Teacher, I am growing very astute at knowing what is happening, and much more proficient than I was at guessing your thoughts."

Sacha stiffened, then without considering her reply she said quickly:

76

"I hope that is . . . untrue."

"Why?" the Duke asked. "What are you hiding that you are afraid of my knowing?"

Realising she had made a mistake Sacha said quickly:

"I think a person's . . . thoughts should . . . always be her . . . own."

"Nonsense!" the Duke replied. "According to your philosophy, which is of course very Greek, what one thinks one becomes. It follows that your thoughts are very important because tomorrow you will be what you think today."

Sacha laughed a little uneasily.

"You are just quoting from that book I read you yesterday."

"Why not?" the Duke enquired. "I was listening attentively, and I found surprisingly it made a lot of common sense."

Because the book in question had been written by her father, Sacha felt that they were on dangerous ground and she tried to turn the subject by saying:

"I am sure it is time I went to change. Your grandmother will be very annoyed if I am late for dinner."

"There is plenty of time," the Duke said drýly, "and I have a suspicion that you are running away from me, though I cannot quite understand why."

Sacha found it hard to give him an answer.

It was yet another occasion when in talking to the Duke she found herself metaphorically 'skating on thin ice.'

When she read the newspapers to him or her father's books he would argue with her on some point, and she found herself responding in the same way as she did in the arguments she had with her father.

Because the subjects were usually those about which

she felt very strongly, and were close to her heart, it was difficult to remember that she should speak as Deirdre and not as herself.

It was even more difficult because she knew that in most cases her cousin would have been uninterested, but would not have had the slightest idea of how to follow the Duke's train of thought.

Sacha had made up her mind this morning that it would be safer to keep to such subjects as the debates in the House of Lords, or the winners of the horse-races which were reported on the sporting pages.

But even these could constitute a danger.

"How can you know so much about the horses owned by my colleagues in the Jockey Club?" the Duke had asked.

"Whether they win or lose is often very important to Papa," Sacha replied.

She was thinking as she spoke of how many people there were in the village who staked the shillings they could ill afford on their favourite horses, and how in consequence unless their children were to go hungry her father often had to put his hand into his own pocket.

Of course he pretended that the money came out of the Church Funds, but as these were lamentably small, Sacha knew this meant that they themselves would not be able to afford a good Sunday luncheon or something they needed for the house would have to wait for several more weeks.

She was thinking of this when the Duke remarked dryly:

"I cannot believe your father, who is a rich man, finds his income affected either by which horse passes the winning-post first or by the turn of a card at the gaming-tables."

Too late Sacha remembered that her Uncle seldom had a bet, and certainly could not by any stretch of the imagination be called a 'gamester.'

There was a little pause before she said somewhat lamely:

"I think...everybody...likes to be a...winner."

"That is true," the Duke admitted. "At the same time, you were speaking as if it was of real consequence in your life who won the Derby or the Grand National Steeplechase."

Because she had no answer to this, Sacha said quickly:

"That is a race I would really like to see, except that I would feel deeply distressed to see the horses fall at the fences in case they were badly hurt."

"Why should the horses matter to you?" the Duke asked.

"Because I love them," Sacha replied simply. "I think nothing is more exciting than riding a well-bred horse and feeling one is being carried as swiftly as the wind."

She was thinking as she spoke of her Uncle's horses which she had been able to ride when she had lessons with Deirdre, and how hard it was to bear, while the stables at the Big House were full, having either to walk, or occasionally being able to ride the slow, aging animal which drew her father's gig.

"Well, once we are married," the Duke said, "you shall have the finest horses that are procurable."

"That would be more wonderful than I can say in words," Sacha answered.

She was dreaming for the moment that what he had promised her might come true, and she was imagining herself galloping beside him when he remarked:

"Before you came here you gave me the impression of being more interested in dancing than in riding."

"I think . . . both are equally . . . enjoyable."

"Of course," the Duke agreed. "At the same time, I shall be very interested to see how you perform as an equestrian."

Sacha drew in her breath.

She remembered too late that Deirdre, while quite a good rider because she had been well taught and had superb horses, was in fact frightened of taking any risks and since she grew up, refused to jump a fence.

"Supposing I fell and scarred my face?" she had said to Sacha. "I know of one girl of about my age who broke her nose out hunting. That is something I am determined will never happen to me."

She therefore insisted on riding only the quietest and best-trained horses, and seldom went faster than a trot.

There were other subjects too in which Sacha found herself floundering and desperately afraid that the Duke would realise that she was an imposter.

Fortunately she had learned that despite the fact that her cousin and the Duke were to be married, they had spent very little time alone together.

They had met mostly at Balls and Receptions in London, and only once had Deirdre visited his huge house in Buckinghamshire and then for only three days when she had been part of a large house-party.

At the same time she was aware that the Duke had as Deirdre had said, thought her the most beautiful girl he had ever seen, and unexpectedly he had confided another reason for their marriage.

"I shall be thirty next birthday," he said, "and the family has been nagging me for some years to get married."

"It was something you did not want to do?" Sacha asked.

"To be frank I hated the idea," he replied, "but I have no brothers, and if anything should happen to me, the Dukedom would go to an obscure cousin who is over sixty, and so far has only produced four daughters."

Sacha thought how tiresome it must be to be the possessor of an important title and be obliged to marry, whether one wanted to or not, in order to produce an heir.

She knew how bitterly her uncle resented the fact that he had a daughter but no sons, and she had often heard her mother saying how sorry she was for her brother.

"Did you and Papa mind that I was a girl?" Sacha had asked.

Her mother laughed.

"We are very proud of our beautiful daughter, and we love her very much," she answered. "While I am sure your papa would have liked a dozen more children, it would have been impossible for us to feed them all. And as you know, there is nothing for them to inherit except for the furniture which grows more shabby every year."

It did not sound as if Lady Margaret minded and when she grew older Sacha had understood that it was the rich aristrocrats with their large estates who were forced into marriage so that they could have sons to inherit what had been handed down from generation to generation.

The Duke interrupted her thoughts.

"You are very quiet! What are you thinking about?"

"I was thinking," she replied truthfully, "that arranged marriages are horrible and unnatural."

She knew if she could have seen his eyes that the Duke would have been looking surprised.

"But that is something which occurs in every Royal family all over Europe, and in most noble families."

"Yes, I know," Sacha agreed.

"Therefore I am very lucky," he said, "because I want to believe that you would have married me if I had just been plain 'Mr. Silchester,' and not a Duke."

Sacha drew in her breath.

She was thinking that Deirdre loved Lord Gerard, and would not for a moment have contemplated marrying the man beside her with the bandage over his eyes unless he had been not only a Duke but an exceedingly rich one.

The Duke put out his hand palm upwards.

"That is true, is it not?" he asked.

As she thought of it as 'doing the right thing,' Sacha slowly and a little reluctantly put her hand in his.

"Yes ... yes ... of ... course."

Because it was a lie and because she was frightened, there was a tremor in her voice, and her fingers fluttered against the Duke's palm.

"Why do you speak like that?" he asked. "You told me you loved me for myself, and I believed you. Have you changed your mind?"

"No ... no! Of course ... not!" Sacha said quickly.

Because she was afraid of what he might be thinking she got to her feet saying:

"You are not to ... worry yourself about ... anything. That is what the Doctors ordered."

"I am not worrying," the Duke said, but he did not release her hand, and she stood captive beside his bed.

"No, I am not worrying," he repeated as if he was thinking it out for himself. "I am just reassuring myself that what you said to me in London was the truth, and that you love me as a man, and not for my rank or my possessions."

"I cannot think," Sacha said, "why you should imagine that what I felt in London should have changed because we are now in Scotland."

"We did not have much time to talk in London," the Duke replied, "and now we can be alone together, I am very interested in what you feel about love, and of course about me."

With difficulty Sacha forced a little laugh.

"Now you are asking for compliments," she said lightly, "and I have always thought they were what women wanted to receive, not men."

"It depends who makes them," the Duke answered. "What do you think of me as a man?"

Because it was impossible to release her hand Sacha sat down again in the chair.

"Do you want the truth, or what you would like to hear?" she asked.

"That is a foolish question," the Duke replied. "I am asking for the truth."

Because his fingers were strong and were holding her prisoner, and because there was something compelling about him she could not resist, Sacha found herself telling him what was in her mind, and for the moment she was not pretending to be Deirdre.

"I think," she said slowly, "that you are well aware that you are of great consequence and that you accept it as your right. But apart from that, you have a critical faculty which you either ignore, or forget to use."

The Duke's fingers tightened sharply as if in surprise.

"What do you mean by that?" he enquired.

"You told me to tell you the truth," Sacha said in a low voice, "and I think that while you are magnificent as a sportsman, and an undisputed social leader among your friends, there are a great many other possibilities about yourself that you have not considered or explored."

There was silence for a moment. Then the Duke said:

"I am naturally waiting to hear what those are."

"I think I have said enough," Sacha replied, "and you can think them out for yourself."

"It is not enough," the Duke objected. "You have challenged me in a way I have never been challenged before, and now I insist that you explain yourself further, and tell me where I am found wanting."

"I have not said . . . that."

"But you insinuated it."

Sacha thought unhappily that she had become involved in a way she had not meant to be.

Yet there was something about the Duke that seemed to force the truth from her, and made it impossible for her just to play lightly and inconsequentially the role she had been allotted.

"I feel . . . perhaps I am being . . . impertinent," she said at length, "and you must forgive me. My only excuse is that as you are well aware . . . it is unusual for me to be . . . alone with somebody like . . . you."

"That was not what you said in London," the Duke replied, "but never mind. Having come so far I am not going to allow you to retreat until I have your explanation of exactly what you mean by what you have just said."

"Very well," Sacha replied almost defiantly. "I have learnt from the way we have talked together that you have an astute and unusually intelligent brain but, like so many other people, you are only using one tenth of it, and that is expended entirely on material things which, while they are enjoyable, have not developed you to your full potential."

She spoke as if the words came to her lips without her asking for them, almost as if they were dictated to her.

Now the Duke released her hand and she knew he was astonished that anybody would speak to him in such a way, and yet at the same time her intuition told her that he knew perceptively that she had spoken the truth.

Because he was silent she was quite certain she had gone too far and that he would be angry.

"I . . . I am . . . sorry."

"Why should you be sorry?" the Duke asked. "I asked you for the truth, and that is what you have given me. I am only surprised—perhaps 'astounded' is a better word—that you should think such things, let alone dare to say what no one else has said since I left Oxford."

The Duke twisted his lips before he added:

"I am beginning to be afraid that you are not only that awesome creature 'a woman with a brain,' but also as I have said before, a Witch!"

"I can only . . . apologise," Sacha said in a low voice, "and you must . . . forgive me because you can see I am very . . . ignorant, and . . . inexperienced in such . . . matters."

"Now *you* are being untruthful," the Duke said accusingly. "I know that what you said to me just now is what you really think, and it is certainly good for my soul, if not for my ego."

"It must not . . . upset you . . . please . . . dismiss it from your . . . mind."

"I have no intention of doing that," the Duke answered. "You have opened up a new vista, or perhaps the right word is 'horizon' which I had forgotten even existed. I have the uncomfortable feeling that everything you have said is right, and I am wasting my capabilities on material things. But I am not quite certain what is the alternative, or for what I should be searching."

As if she could not help herself, Sacha said quickly:

"What I feel you should ask yourself, as an undoubted leader, is where you are taking those who follow you, and what goal lies ahead."

As if once again she was afraid she had said too much she rose to say:

"I promised your grandmother I would have tea with her, and I am sure she is waiting for me."

"No, do not leave me!" the Duke ordered, but she pretended not to hear him and slipped away from his bedroom without saying any more.

Only when she went to her own room to tidy before tea did she ask herself how she could have been so stupid as to become involved in such a conversation!

She was afraid she had not only endangered her own position with the Duke, but might have made things difficult for Deirdre in the future.

At the same time she had known that every moment she was with him she had been forcibly aware of how clever and quick-witted he was beneath his facade of indifference to everything but sport and the Social World in which he and Deirdre shone so brightly.

Sacha sighed.

'I suppose it was Papa who made me aware,' she thought, 'that we have so much to give to the world, if we use our intelligence and reach towards the Divine.'

Those were her father's ideas and hers, but she was sure that the Duke was entirely content with his life as it was, and she had no right to interfere or interrupt it.

And yet she could feel as she sat beside him vibrations coming from him which told her he exuded a power that was greater than himself.

Her father would have said it was the Divine Life Force pouring through him. But Sacha knew that it was not enough for the power to be within a person: it had to be directed and used, and that was what the Duke was not doing.

Now she thought she had made a great mistake.

"How could I have been so . . . stupid as not to . . . leave things as they . . . are?" she asked herself, "and accept him as he is for the short time I am here? Why should I try to change him?"

She told herself it was because she admired him so much, and because she was aware that he was the most vital person she had ever met, she could not bear him to fall short of his own ideals.

'They are there with . . . him,' she thought, 'but until he is aware of them. they will lie dormant and useless, and therefore lost to the world which needs them.'

"Why should that matter to you?" a voice asked as if it was her conscience speaking.

Because she was afraid of the answer she quickly left her bedroom to run down the passage towards the Drawing-Room where she knew the Duchess would be.

She was there, and as Sacha entered the big room she put down the embroidery on which she had been working and rose to her feet.

"I was just wondering, my dear, if you were coming to have tea with me," she said, "but I did not wish to interrupt you and Talbot."

"I think he has had enough of my company for the moment," Sacha replied, and the Duchess laughed.

"I am sure that is not true! You have made him so much happier since you arrived and that will make all the difference to his chances of a quick recovery."

"I do hope . . . so."

"I promise you he is a different person since you have been here with him. Tomkins, who knows him so well, says you are far better than any Doctor, despite those strange concoctions you make him drink!"

Sacha laughed.

"I am afraid, both Tomkins and your Cook are very

sceptical about their doing any good, but I like to believe they will strengthen his eyes and when they take off the bandages, he will see quite clearly again."

"That is what we all pray will happen," the Duchess said quietly, as they walked towards the room where the tea had been laid.

When Sacha returned to the Duke's bedroom the Duchess went with her, and it was only when she left them to change for dinner that the Duke had asked Sacha to come back again later.

"I wish he could see me in these gowns," Sacha murmured to herself as she looked at first one, then another, and found it difficult to decide which would be the most becoming.

Then she remembered that if the Duke could see her it would be disastrous.

While he could be deceived into believing while they were talking that she was Deirdre, he would certainly know immediately as soon as he could see her, that there were unmistakable differences even though they were cousins and had the same colouring.

"I would have to leave anyway before he can see again," Sacha told herself, "and actually I have only two days left."

She had not told him when she had to leave, and now when she remembered it, it seemed as if the time of her stay at the Castle was flying by on wings and soon, like for Cinderella, midnight would strike and she would be back in her outgrown and threadbare gowns in the Vicarage.

It was hard not to believe that the beautiful clothes which Deirdre had given her would not vanish too: but, even if they remained, what would be the use of them?

There would be no one to notice what she was wearing

and no one like the Duke to talk to.

She wondered why there seemed to be a sudden aching pain in her breast and that the setting sun over the moors had changed to a grey mist.

Then she told herself she was being very ungrateful.

How could she have guessed a few days ago that she would enjoy this marvellous adventure of coming to Scotland, of being dressed like a Princess and being able to talk, argue and duel in words with the most interesting man she had ever known in her whole life?

Although at first she had been very frightened, the enchantment of it had grown hour by hour until when she awoke she was counting the minutes until she could go to the Duke's room, and Tomkins would hand her the newspapers for her to read to him.

At other times there was the Castle to explore, the gardens to admire, the beauty of the moorlands and the lake to look at. It all entranced her until she felt she had in fact, stepped into a fairyland which had no existence except in her imagination.

"I am so lucky, so unbelievably lucky," she told herself "and nobody suspects for one moment that I am not who I am pretending to be."

At the same time, as she changed for dinner she warned herself that she must be very careful of what she said to the Duke.

'I shall have to tell Deirdre what I have discussed with him,' she thought and shivered as she realised that Deirdre would be very angry with her.

In the past Deirdre had often scoffed at what she called her cousin's 'airy-fairy ideas.'

"I like practical things," she had said once, "and if you want the truth, Sacha, I am not in the least interested in my soul, or what happens to me in the next world.

I want to enjoy this one, to be acclaimed as a beauty and to marry the most important man in England."

Deirdre, she thought, had certainly succeeded in all her ambitions, and yet something within herself which she could not ignore told Sacha that Deirdre was missing something exquisite, ecstatic, that was far more important than anything else.

She knew that she had touched the fringe of it herself when she looked at a lovely view, when she heard music, and also when she prayed.

She had the feeling, although she was not quite sure, that it was something that could be summed up in one word, which was 'love.'

"I'm ever so glad you're wearing that gown, M'Lady," Emily exclaimed interrupting her thoughts.

"Why do you say that?" Sacha asked.

She looked at herself in the long mirror as Emily buttoned her up the back.

"I always thinks it's the prettiest one in Her Ladyship's wardrobe," Emily explained, "but it's one she never liked, and only wore once."

"I wonder why she did not like it?" Sacha asked.

She thought it impossible for anybody not to admire the gown which was of white silk with a lace bertha off the shoulders embroidered with silver and pearls.

The wide crinoline was of white and silver and the same lace ornamented the hem of it.

It made Sacha feel as if she was part of the moon which would soon be rising over the moors to shine on the Castle and give it a magical beauty.

"I thinks Her Ladyship was annoyed because the dressmaker put pearls in amongst the silver instead of them stones what looks like diamonds," Emily was saying. "Her Ladyship was always one for glitter."

"I think it is very beautiful as it is," Sacha said, "and I am very, very lucky to have it."

If Deirdre had only worn it once, it was more than likely that the same thing would be true of her. Where else would it be appropriate for her to wear such a lovely gown?

Her father would be astonished as they sat down at their frugal supper if she wore anything so elaborate!

For the moment however, she was content to walk gracefully down the corridor towards the Drawing-Room, seeing glimpses of herself in the many long gilt-framed mirrors, and knowing that she looked exactly right in the Castle with its fine furniture, high ceilings and portraits of the Duchess's distinguished ancestors.

She entered the Drawing-Room and the Duchess, who had changed into an evening-gown of mauve silk, exclaimed:

"How lovely you look, dearest child! And very like a bride!"

Then before Sacha could reply she went on:

"I feel I am being remiss in not asking people here to meet you, for I know many of our relatives and friends would be only too thrilled to do so. But Talbot was so anxious that his condition should be kept a secret."

"Oh, please," Sacha said quickly, "I am very happy to be with you, and I am sure it is best for nobody to know that the Duke has been injured."

"I agree it would be a mistake," the Duchess said. "Talbot would hate there to be any publicity in the newspapers."

"Then please let us keep it a secret," Sacha said pleadingly.

"Of course I will do exactly what you and Talbot want," the Duchess conceded.

The Butler announced dinner, and half-way through the delicious meal a Piper walked round the table playing the bagpipes which Sacha found exciting and much more interesting than any conversation with strangers would have been.

Only when they went back to the Drawing-Room did the Duchess say:

"I hope you will not think me rude, dear child, if I retire to bed early. It is something I always do, and I also have a slight headache which tells me I need to rest."

"Please do not stay up on my account," Sacha said, "and I promised to go and say goodnight to the Duke, if you do not think that too unconventional."

The Duchess laid her hand on her shoulder.

"I think that you and Talbot getting to know each other is the best thing that could possibly happen," she said. "I have always thought it a mistake for two people to marry before they know each other well and have become real friends."

She smiled as she added:

"Perhaps your mother might think that I was being a somewhat negligent chaperon, but that will have to be another secret we will keep to ourselves."

They walked along the passage, and the Duchess kissed her before she went to her room while Sacha walked on alone towards the Duke's.

Tomkins let her in saying:

"I don't think you oughta stop long, M'Lady. His Grace is tired though he won't admit it, and he should get all the sleep he can before the next operation."

"Yes, of course," Sacha agreed, "and I have no wish to overtire him."

Tomkins opened the second door which led into the

Duke's bedroom and as she went in she saw that the curtains had been drawn, and there were candelabra holding lighted candles on each side of the huge four-poster bed.

"I have been waiting for you," the Duke said reproachfully as she walked towards the bed.

"We have only just finished dinner," Sacha said, "and it was very exciting for me to hear the pipes."

"Did you really enjoy them, or do you think them hideous as most Sassenachs do?" the Duke asked.

"Now you are insulting me," Sacha replied. "I think the music of the pipes is as beautiful as Scotland itself. They are also inspiring and stimulating."

The Duke gave a little laugh.

"I think once again you are preaching to me."

"No, no, I promise you I am not doing that," Sacha replied.

She had reached the side of the bed and was standing near him and he said:

"If the pipes inspire and stimulate you, that is what you do to me."

"I wish that were true," Sacha said. "It is the nicest compliment you could possibly pay me."

"I should have thought that like most women you would wish to hear a eulogy to your eyes, your skin and of course your hair."

"Now you are spoiling what is something I shall always treasure."

"I doubt it, seeing how many compliments to your beauty you have received," the Duke said dryly.

Sacha did not reply.

She wondered what he would say if she told him she had never received any compliments, and therefore what he had just said was something very precious that she would put away in her memory to take out whenever she felt sad or depressed.

The Duke held out his hand towards her and said:

"Come nearer, I want to know what you are wearing."

"It is very beautiful," Sacha said, "the most beautiful gown I possess."

"What colour is it?"

"It is white and silver, and it makes me think of the loch and the moon which soon will be rising in the sky."

There was a rapt note again in her voice and after a moment the Duke said:

"I want to feel it."

She came nearer still, and as he put out his hand to touch the fullness of her skirt she sat down on the edge of the mattress.

"I wish I could see you."

"You will soon," Sacha said reassuringly.

Then because she did not wish him to worry about his eyes she said:

"Feel the bertha. It is so pretty. It is made of lace embroidered with silver and little pearls."

She took his hand as she spoke and put his fingers on the wide lace bertha, and as he touched it he said:

"Do the pearls have the same translucence as your skin?"

"I . . . I hope so."

His fingers moved from the bertha up to her bare shoulder. His touch was very light, and yet it gave Sacha a strange sensation she could not explain.

"I am right," the Duke said, "but your skin has a warmth beneath it which the pearls lack."

He moved his fingers over her shoulder and touched her neck.

She wore no necklace and slowly the Duke raised his hand a little higher until he spread his fingers out to encircle the round column beneath her chin.

It was then that Sacha felt as if little shafts of moon-light were running through her breasts. It was a sensation she had never known, and yet at the same time it was very exciting.

The moonlight seemed to ripple through her whole body, and it was difficult to breathe.

The Duke's other arm went round her and he pulled her near to him as he said:

"I have not kissed you since you came here because I thought that with my eyes bandaged you might find me repulsive. But now I want to kiss you more than I have ever wanted it before."

Because his tone was low and deep and his fingers still encircled her neck Sacha felt as though her voice was lost. All she could think of was the moonlight invading her breast, moving up her throat until it touched her lips.

Then as she knew he should not kiss her and it was something she should not allow, it was too late.

The Duke pulled her down, and as she lay helpless in his arms his lips came down on hers.

For a moment she could hardly believe it was happening, until the touch of his mouth and the insistence of it told her it was real.

It was impossible to move, impossible too to think of anything except that the moonlight within her seemed to move her whole being irresistibly towards the Duke.

His arms tightened, his lips became more demanding, more possessive, and she felt that the wild beating of her heart was echoed by his.

He kissed her until she felt as if he carried her up into the sky and the moonlight within her merged with the light from him.

It was so exquisite, so perfect, that she knew that this was what she had always sought. It was, as she had felt earlier in the evening, the love that was more important than anything else in the world.

The Duke kissed her until he drew her heart from her body and made it his.

Only when he raised his head did Sacha make an inarticulate little murmur and hide her face against his neck.

For a moment he held her very close. Then he said:

"And now you must go to bed, my darling."

As if she awoke from a dream Sacha managed to move from his arms, and he made no effort to stop her.

As she stood beside him looking down, knowing that her whole body was throbbing with the sensations he had aroused in her, he reached out and felt for her hand, and taking it in his raised it to his lips.

"Dream of me," he said in his deep voice, "and I shall be thinking of you."

Sacha tried to speak, but it was impossible.

She could only look at the movement of his lips, knowing that the kiss he had given her had been the most wonderful thing that had ever happened and was at the moment beyond thought, beyond understanding.

Then because it was so ecstatic and there were no words in which she could express what she felt, she slipped her hand from his and running blindly across the room opened the door.

Tomkins was waiting outside, but she did not speak to him.

She hurried away down the passage and only when

she reached her own room did she stand with her back to the closed door fighting for breath, knowing at the same time that her whole world had changed.

Never had she envisaged in her wildest dreams that she could feel like this. She was disembodied, flying in the sky, yet pulsating with very human emotions that were an ecstasy beyond words.

This was love; a love so perfect, so spiritual that it could only be part of God, and yet it was centred on earth in one man, the Duke, who was to marry her cousin Deirdre.

chapter five

SACHA awoke and knew she had not only dreamt of the Duke, but had thought of him for a very long time before she went to sleep.

Her whole body had seemed to come alive with the wonder of his kiss, and she knew that now she had found love it was even more wonderful, more ecstatic and more sacred than she had imagined.

Her mind seemed to be reaching out towards the sky, and she knew that incredibly, although it was difficult to believe it, she had given him her heart and soul.

"How can I have been so foolish, so absurd," she asked herself, "when he belongs to Deirdre?"

Then it was an additional and unexpected agony to remember that to Deirdre he was just a Duke and not the man she loved.

"I love . . . him! I . . . love him!" Sacha said to herself.

As if she must share her feelings with the beauty outside, she jumped out of bed and went to the window to pull back the curtains.

The sun had just risen, and once again there was a wonderful light on the moors and the loch was like a silver mirror beneath a cloudless sky.

It was so exquisite that it became part of her love, and she knew whatever happened in the future she would never be able to forget the ecstasy of last night which had somehow merged with the beauty of Scotland itself.

Emily came to call her and was surprised to find her up.

"You're early this morning, M'Lady!" she exclaimed. "Everybody downstairs was saying how beautiful your gown was last night."

Her words brought back the feeling when the Duke, having felt her bertha with his fingers, moved them to her shoulder, and Sacha felt herself quiver again as she had when he touched her.

She dressed slowly, hardly aware of what she was doing, conscious only that as the minutes ticked by she would soon be with the Duke.

Sometimes the Duchess came down to breakfast, but if she was too tired Sacha ate alone.

She entered the Dining-Room to find there was nobody there except for the Butler to wait on her, and because she thought it was expected, she ate a little porridge before she sampled the delicious dishes that were so different from what Nanny cooked at the Vicarage.

There was speckled trout which Sacha knew had come from the burns, salmon fish-cakes, eggs encircled by mushrooms, and a home-cured ham, so that it was difficult to choose what she would most enjoy!

When she left the table she thought guiltily that she had eaten too much.

"If only I were a camel," she told herself, "when I return home I would not want to eat for at least a week, and that would save money."

She only wished she could take some of the delicious food that was provided at the Castle back to her father, and thought how surprised both the Duchess and the Duke would be if she told them how at the Vicarage they were often hungry when they were too short of money to pay for what they ate.

Then her thoughts were back again with the Duke, and it was impossible to think of anything but him.

She knew there was no chance of seeing him until he was washed and shaved, his bed had been made, and Tomkins had served his breakfast.

She therefore went downstairs and out into the garden. It was so warm that she had no need of a wrap, and the breeze was soft against her cheeks and barely strong enough to untidy her hair.

She walked round looking at the flowers and thinking in some strange way that each one of them was a part of her feelings for the Duke.

Then at last, when she felt as if a century rather than an hour had passed, she went back to the Castle, hoping the Duke would be ready for her.

Instead she found the Duchess had just come from her bedroom.

"Good morning, my dear," she said. "I am sorry I was too tired this morning to join you at breakfast, but now I want to speak to you."

The way she spoke made Sacha look at her apprehensively, and they went into the Drawing-Room with its four long stone-framed windows overlooking the garden and with a very beautiful portrait of the Duchess painted when she was young over the huge mantelpiece.

Because Sacha sensed there was something wrong she looked at the Dowager with worried eyes as she settled herself in her usual chair by the fireplace.

"I heard this morning," she began, "from our local Doctor that the two Specialists who will be attending my grandson will be arriving tomorrow morning."

Sacha stiffened, then asked:

"Two Specialists?"

"Yes, dear," the Duchess replied. "One is the Surgeon who will operate to remove the last piece of metal that is in his body, and the other is, of course, the Eye Specialist."

"You mean," Sacha asked, "that they intend to take off his bandages?"

"Yes, dear, and we can only hope that our prayers have been heard, and that dear Talbot will be able to see again."

She saw the look of consternation on Sacha's face and said:

"Do not look so worried. I have told you that I am clairvoyant, and I am quite certain that Talbot is so strong and so much better in every way since you have been here that the Specialists will have good news for us."

Sacha did not speak and the Duchess went on:

"They are arriving together because they are close friends and although I should have thought an interval between the operation and the removal of Talbot's bandages might have been a good thing, I am quite certain that after they have attended to my grandson they will expect to spend the day fishing before they return South."

The Duchess smiled before she said:

"One thing that makes me very happy is that you seem to like Scotland so much. I was so afraid that Talbot would marry one of those Society girls who would always want to be in London, and I can assure you it is a great relief to know that you like the country as much as he does."

It was difficult for Sacha not to reply that she had seldom been to London, and the country was her home and very much part of herself.

Because she knew it would please the Duchess, she said:

"I do not think there could be anybody who would not love anything as beautiful as this Castle and the moors."

"That is what I like to hear you say," the Duchess smiled. "And now I will let you into a secret which even Talbot does not know: I have left the Castle and all the land I possess to him in my will. He has always been my favourite grandson, and I know it will please him to spend some part of the year here, and that he will look after my people as if he were as Scottish as I am."

"I know that will...thrill him when he...knows about it," Sacha said in a low voice.

It was agonising to know that she would never be at the Castle with the Duke and he would never teach her to fish as he had promised to do.

She was also quite certain that if he did come to Scotland he would come alone because Deirdre would want to be in London.

"So many young women," the Duchess went on, "have 'set their caps' as the saying goes, at Talbot, which is not surprising, seeing how attractive he is. But he always managed to resist them until he saw you."

She paused before she continued:

"Even then I was worried when I heard how beautiful you were and what a success in London. I feel because I am 'fey' that Talbot needs a very different type of wife to make him happy, and persuade him to do all the things he is capable of doing, and to help other people rather than just enjoy himself."

Because that was just what she had thought herself, Sacha stared at the Duchess in surprise as she continued:

"But since you have come here, I know you not only have made Talbot better, but at the same time have made him think in a way he has not done before."

"How can you know that?" Sacha asked, knowing that when she was alone with the Duke there had been no one to overhear their conversation.

The Duchess smiled.

"I think I knew it instinctively, but when I realised you were reading to him that very interesting book called *The Light of Greece* I knew it was a very different type of literature from anything Talbot has read in the past."

Sacha gave a little exclamation of delight.

She was just about to say: "How wonderful that you have read my father's book!" when she remembered that she was supposed to be Deirdre—who found any book a bore unless it was a love-story.

As if following the train of her own thoughts the Duchess went on:

"I have often longed to meet the Reverend Mervyn Waverley and once or twice I thought of writing to him, but I am quite certain he would think it an impertinence, and I expect anyway that he lives in the South."

"I am sure any author would be very . . . proud to think that his . . . work pleased you," Sacha said, choosing her words with care.

"Then perhaps one day I will be brave enough to tell him how much I have enjoyed the two books he has written. I do hope he will soon write more, if he is still alive."

With difficulty Sacha prevented herself from saying that her father was very much alive, and certainly would be delighted to know that anybody as distinguished as the Duchess found his books enjoyable.

"I suppose I should blame myself," the Duchess went on, "for not suggesting to Talbot that he should read *The Light of Greece*. However, I think the reason I refrained from doing so was that it meant so much to me personally that I could not bear that anybody, not even my dearest grandson, should disparage it or fail to understand the message it contained."

She smiled at Sacha again before she added:

"That is another thing you and I have in common, my dear, not only our love for dear Talbot, but for Greece and the light it has given to the world."

"It is wonderful of you to understand," Sacha exclaimed.

"I am very old," the Duchess said. "I shall not live very much longer, but I want you to know that it has given me great happiness to have you here and to know that Talbot's future is in the hands of just the sort of wife I would have chosen for him had he asked me to do so."

Because the way she spoke was so moving, and because Sacha not only felt the tears prick her eyes, but had also a feeling of guilt that was almost a physical pain, she jumped up from the Duchess's side and walked to the window.

She stood with her back to the room not seeing the view in front of her, but only a desolate and barren future without the Duke.

Then as if the words came to her lips without her conscious volition, she asked:

"S—suppose I . . . fail him?"

The Duchess gave a little laugh.

"Like everybody in love you feel that you are not good enough for the person to whom you have given your heart, but I know you will not fail Talbot and he will not fail you. I can see it as clearly as if the future was pictured before me."

"You are . . . wrong! You are wrong!" Sacha wanted to cry, but instead, because she could not bear to hurt the Duchess, she went back to her side to say:

"Thank you for all the kind and sweet things you have said to me. They mean more than I can ever tell you, and I shall never . . . forget."

There was a little throb in her voice which told the Duchess she was suffering, and she put out her hand.

"I know, dearest Child, you are worrying about Talbot," she said, "but there is no need. Just make him believe that everything will be well. You and I know that in every crisis in life it is important to have the will to win."

"I will . . . do my . . . best," Sacha answered.

*   *   *

Half an hour later she heard the Duke was ready to see her, and as she hurried towards his bedroom she found Tomkins waiting for her in the passage outside the outer door.

"His Grace is ready for me?" she asked.

"Yes, M'Lady," Tomkins replied, "but there's something I wants to say to Your Ladyship."

"What is it?" Sacha asked apprehensively.

"His Grace has heard that them doctors be coming tomorrow to cut him up and take off his bandages, and it's something he's not looking forward to."

"I can understand that."

"I thinks if the truth's known, M'Lady," Tomkins

went on, "it's his eyes His Grace be a-worrying about most."

"I am sure he will be all right," Sacha answered.

"Then you make him believe it, M'Lady," Tomkins said almost fiercely. "I've been with His Grace for many years, and I've served with him in the Army. Brave as a lion he was against the enemy, afraid of nothing, but blindness be another thing all together."

"Yes, of course it is," Sacha agreed, "and I will help him all I can. You know I will."

"Make him believe, M'Lady," Tomkins said, "that it doesn't matter to you one way or the other if he can see or not. That's all he wants to know."

The way Tomkins spoke made Sacha feel as if she were listening to Nanny, and she knew he was worrying over the Duke as if he were a small boy in pain.

"I will help him," she said, "I promise you I will."

"That's what I wanted to hear, M'Lady," Tomkins replied, and without saying any more he walked ahead of her to open the two doors which led into the Duke's bedroom.

He was sitting up in bed and Sacha thought despite his bandages he looked very handsome and authoritative. At the same time she knew perceptively that just as she would have felt in the same circumstances, there was a nasty little feeling of fear moving within him.

She walked towards the bed and he said abruptly:

"I suppose you have heard what is going to happen tomorrow?"

Because the mere sight of him had brought back the ecstasy that he had given her last night and she could feel the rapture of it sweeping through her once again, Sacha found it hard to answer him in what she hoped was a normal voice.

"Your grandmother has told me," she said, "and I

think you must be glad, as I am, to know that you will not have to go on...waiting any...longer. There is nothing...worse than...waiting and...worrying."

"Who said I was worrying?" the Duke asked harshly.

Sacha stood beside him and because she could not help it she put out her hand and laid it on his. His fingers tightened on hers until it was painful.

Then in a voice that did not sound like his own he said:

"I *am*—afraid!"

"No, no, you must not be!" Sacha said quickly. "Because you are so strong there is really nothing to fear."

"I am not afraid of the pain," the Duke replied, "or of the operation, but only of being blind and losing you."

Sacha drew in her breath.

The way the Duke had spoken the last words made a little tremor run through her which she could not suppress.

"You will not...lose me," she said softly. "I know in my...heart that you will see again...but if you are...unable to do so...then it will make no...difference."

The Duke's fingers tightened until Sacha's were bloodless. Then he asked:

"Do you mean that? Do you really mean it?"

"I mean...it."

There was however just a faint hesitation before she spoke because it flashed through her mind that Deirdre would indeed mind! Deirdre would not wish to be married to a blind man.

Almost as if he realised what she was thinking the Duke said:

"Do you swear to me on everything you hold holy that if when they take off my bandages I cannot see, you

108

will still marry me, even though it means leading me about like a dog for the rest of my life?"

Because the pain in his voice was so obvious and Sacha could not bear to hear it, she said quickly:

"I swear that I will...stay with you and...look after...you."

Even as she spoke she thought despairingly that she had committed Deirdre to a life she would find unendurable, but there was nothing she could do except to reply as she had done.

The Duke gave a sigh that seemed to come from the depths of his being. Then he asked:

"If you really mean what you say, I have something to suggest to you."

The way he spoke made Sacha apprehensive and she asked:

"What is...it?"

"It is something I thought of after you left me last night," the Duke said, "but I was afraid to suggest it to you."

"There is no...need to be...afraid."

Because he was still holding her hand so tightly and they were so near to each other, it was hard to think of anything but the wonder of his lips on hers and the way in which he had carried her up to the sky and made her feel as if the moonlight was shining through her.

"Because I believe you love me," the Duke said, "I am going to ask you if you will marry me before I am operated on tomorrow and before the bandages are taken from my eyes!"

She felt his fingers tighten on hers and knew that even without being able to see he must have been aware that she was staring at him wide-eyed.

"I...I do not...understand."

The Duke smiled for the first time since she had come into the room.

"In Scotland, my darling," he said, "there is a very easy way by which we can be married secretly without anybody being aware of it."

"S—secretly?" Sacha repeated, thinking that what he was saying must be just a figment of her imagination.

The Duke pulled her a little nearer to him.

"Sit down on the bed as you did last night," he said, "and I will tell you what I have planned, if you agree."

Feeling as if once again she had stepped into a dream, Sacha did as he told her.

He lifted her hand to his lips.

At the touch of his mouth on her skin she felt not the moonlight but a flame of the burning sun sweeping through her breasts and her breath came quickly through her parted lips.

"Now I know that you really love me," the Duke said, "I want you, my precious one, to agree to what I suggest, just in case we are being over-optimistic and I die on the operating-table."

"I know you ... will not do ... that," Sacha said unsteadily.

"No one can be quite certain," the Duke replied, "and the piece of metal which has to be removed is near my heart. That is why I have had to keep quiet and stay in bed just in case it moved. It was also at first very inflamed."

"How ... terrible!" Sacha exclaimed. "Why did you not ... tell me ... before?"

"I had no wish to talk about it," the Duke answered. "But because it is a sensible thing to do, I have made a will in which I have left everything I possess personally, apart from the estates and the houses which are entailed onto the next Duke, to my wife."

"I . . . I do not wish you to do . . . that," Sacha said quickly. "Please . . . forget it. If you were . . . dead I could not . . . bear to benefit . . . from it in any . . . way."

"That is just what I would expect you to say," the Duke said in a deep voice, "but even if I do not die, which I agree seems at the moment unlikely, I may be blind. Then, my darling, I should be a tiresome encumbrance to you unless you love me enough to believe I can go on 'seeing' as you have taught me to do by the light in which the Greeks believed."

"That you will . . . always be . . . able to do."

"Not unless you are there to help me to believe, and to sustain and comfort me," the Duke insisted.

Because she knew he was again really asking a question, Sacha found herself, because she could not bear to disappoint him, saying:

"You know I . . . will do . . . that. You know . . . that I . . . love you!"

"I wanted to be sure, to be absolutely sure!" the Duke said. "That is why I am going to ask you to marry me secretly under Scottish Law and nobody will know anything about it unless I die."

"I . . . I do not . . . understand," Sacha said again.

"Let me explain," the Duke said. "To take charge of my will I have sent for a very old friend to come and see me this afternoon. He is older than I am, but we have often enjoyed fishing together, and he is now the Sheriff of this County."

Sacha was listening and watching the Duke's lips as he spoke.

At the same time she felt as though her head was filled with cotton wool and it was almost impossible to understand what he was saying to her.

"When the Sheriff is here," the Duke went on, "You have only to agree in front of him that we are married and we will be. In Scotland it is called *'Marriage by Consent'* or *'Irregular Marriage'* but it is completely binding and legal."

The Duke paused. Then he said:

"And that, my precious one, is what I am asking of you, so that I can be sure that whatever happens tomorrow you will be mine."

He ceased speaking and Sacha sat in an astonished silence.

It flashed through her mind that because she loved him it was a request very easily granted.

But how could she explain to Deirdre? How could she possibly tell her cousin that she had been forced into a position in which she could not refuse to do what the Duke asked of her?

As if her silence perplexed him, he said:

"Is it too much to ask? After all, as I have told you, no one will know, and later we will be married in Church with all our friends and relations present, with a Bishop to take the Service, a choir to sing an anthem, and a dozen bridesmaids if you want them to follow you up the aisle."

He spoke with just a slight note of contempt in his voice, as if he thought such ostentation was quite unnecessary. But Sacha knew it was what Deirdre would expect and enjoy, and would certainly not feel married without it.

Then because she knew she had to say something she answered in a low, frightened little voice:

"You . . . you are quite . . . certain that what we do will be . . . secret . . . and no one will . . . know?"

"I swear to you that no one will know except for the

112

Sheriff," the Duke said, "and of course you and me. I know you are worrying as to what your Father and Mother will think, but when we go South you shall have your engagement party as you planned, and of course a traditional wedding with all its trappings."

"I was not . . . thinking of . . . that," Sacha said, "but that perhaps it would be . . . wrong to do anything that is . . . secret."

"The only thing that could be wrong," the Duke replied, "is if you do not love me enough. You have said you will still love me even if I am blind, but are you leaving yourself a loophole so that if the worst comes to the worst, you can be free?"

Now there was a bitterness in the Duke's voice which Sacha found unbearable.

"No, no . . . it is . . . not that at all!" she cried. "It is just that it . . . seems such a . . . big step to take and I suppose I am . . . frightened of being so . . . adventurous."

"You are frightened?" the Duke asked. "That I do not believe, and you have told me that I must take the initiative and use my intelligence in a way I have never done before."

He paused before he said slowly:

"It is that intelligence, perhaps rather than my intuition my darling, which tells me that I must make certain I do not lose you."

To lose her in fact was inevitable, Sacha thought despairingly.

Then suddenly, as if the fog that seemed to encompass her mind cleared, she knew that because she loved him she could not fail him.

What did it matter if Deirdre had to pretend to have married him secretly before they had a big wedding ceremony with all their relations and friends present?

The only thing that was of real importance was that the Duke should go through his operation believing in her love, and being certain in his heart that if he was blind for life she would stay by him and look after him.

It was as if Sacha stood on the top of a cliff and had to take only one step forward to plunge into the sea below. And yet to refuse would be to destroy the Duke's faith in her.

She drew in her breath.

"If that is what you...want me to do," she said in a very small voice, "then...of course I will...do it."

"You mean that? You really mean it?" he asked.

"I mean it."

He gave a cry that was almost a shout as he said:

"You love me, you really love me! I knew it last night when I kissed you, but I thought I must have been dreaming. But now, my precious, you have proved your love, and I swear I will never let you regret it."

As he spoke he put his arms around her, swept her against him, and once again he was kissing her with fiercely passionate lips that made her tremble against him.

Even as the ecstasy he had evoked in her last night was again throbbing through her there came a knock at the door.

Hastily Sacha disengaged herself from the Duke's arms and moved to the chair at the side of the bed.

"Come in!" the Duke said sharply.

It was Tomkins.

"Sorry to disturb Your Grace," he said, "but I've brought you the newspapers."

"Thank you, Tomkins," the Duke said. "Put them down on the bed."

"Also, Your Grace," Tomkins went on, "Dr. Macpherson is here and wants to talk to you about tomorrow."

Sacha rose to leave.

"I will leave you," she said.

"The Sheriff will be here at four o'clock this afternoon," the Duke said in a low voice. "Come to me then unless you change your mind."

"I shall not do . . . that."

Sacha was finding it hard to speak because of the feelings he had aroused in her, and she longed for him to kiss her again.

As she left the room she found Dr. Macpherson, who was the local Physician, waiting outside.

"I think you must be Lady Deirdre Lang," he said, holding out his hand. "Her Grace has been telling me how much you have helped her grandson since you have been staying here."

Because she felt she had to know the truth, Sacha asked:

"How bad will the operation tomorrow be, for His Grace?"

"I am not really worried," Dr. Macpherson replied. "I am confidently sure everything will be 'plain sailing.' The Surgeon could not remove the piece of metal that is near the heart until the swelling had gone down. After visiting His Grace three days ago I wrote at once to London to say that everything seemed in order, and the sooner the last piece was removed the better."

"And . . . his eyes?"

"That is a very different thing," Dr. Macpherson answered. "Eyes are not my province, and we can only hope the injuries, which looked extremely unpleasant at first, have now subsided and left no permanent damage."

"But there is the . . . chance that . . . His Grace will be . . . blind?"

"I would not like to predict the outcome one way or the other," Dr. Macpherson replied evasively, "but Sir Colin Knowles, who is the leading authority on eyes in the whole country, will reveal the truth when he takes off His Grace's bandages."

"That will be . . . after the operation to . . . remove the metal?"

"Yes it will," Dr. Macpherson agreed. "But the two Specialists are travelling here together because they are such friends! Also I think His Grace has been in suspense long enough and would rather know what the future holds for him, one way or another."

"Yes, I am sure that is right," Sacha said. "Thank you, Doctor, for being so frank."

Because she could not bear to hear any more she turned and walked away feeling as if the world had suddenly turned upside-down and she was not certain what she could do about it.

Because she had to think, she did not try to find the Duchess, but went down a side staircase out into the garden, but even there it was difficult to think clearly.

How, she asked herself, could she possibly marry the Duke secretly? And yet how could she refuse?

It was impossible to think of anything else before luncheon, or during the meal which she had alone with the Duchess, or afterwards when she knew the Duke was resting as Tomkins insisted he should.

Time moved on slowly but relentlessly towards the moment when she would marry him.

Then it seemed almost as if her mother was beside her, telling her that love was more important than anything else.

She loved him and therefore she must help him.

It meant, Sacha knew, that she would be married to

him while he would always believe that he was married to Deirdre.

She would never be able to marry anybody else without feeling she was breaking the most sacred vow that any woman could make.

But if she had to sacrifice herself, at least it was in the name of love, and with every breath she drew she knew she loved the Duke more and more.

She could not explain how she did so, though knowing that he was thinking of her as somebody else.

She only knew that the feelings he had aroused in her even before he had kissed her were so rapturous, at the same time so sacred and beautiful, that they were part of the light in which she had always believed and which, as she had taught him, radiated through everyone, although in some more clearly than in others.

The light of Greece—the light of life—the light that came from God—could all be summed up in one word—Love.

* * *

At a quarter to four, when Sacha knew Tomkins would have drawn back the Duke's curtains and he would be ready and waiting for her, she went along to his room.

Although he could not see her, she had put on one of the prettiest gowns that Deirdre had given her and she knew she had never looked more attractive or worn anything which became her better.

Tomkins let her into the bedroom and as she walked towards the Duke she felt almost as if he was watching her approaching him, with a look of admiration in his eyes.

She reached the side of the bed to say in a small voice:

"I . . . I am . . . here."

"I know that," he answered. "I have been waiting for you. Do you still love me, my darling?"

He spoke in a voice which made Sacha's heart turn over in her breast.

"Yes . . . I love you!"

"Enough to marry me?"

"If . . . if that is . . . what you want."

"I want it more than I have ever wanted anything in my whole life!"

As he spoke the Duke put out his hand, and as Sacha put hers into it he said:

"You are frightened, my sweet. There is no need to be. This will be our secret, and ours alone. Whatever happens in the future, I will look after you and love you! You will be mine, and nobody shall take you from me."

Because it was difficult to find words in which to reply Sacha's fingers only tightened on his, and as if he understood the Duke raised her hand to his lips.

The door opened and Tomkins said:

"Sheriff Gordon to see you, Your Grace!"

Sacha turned her head to see a tall, good-looking man whose hair was just beginning to turn grey at the temples come into the room.

He was wearing the Gordon tartan and looked very resplendent as he walked towards the bed.

"What have you been doing to yourself, Talbot?" he asked. "The Duchess has just been telling me that you have had an accident. I cannot think why I was not informed."

"I had no wish for anybody to learn of my stupidity," the Duke replied. "I walked over a part of the moor where no one expected me to go and a gun-trap blew up in my face."

The Sheriff clasped his hand.

"I am sorry to hear about this, more sorry than I can possibly say."

"I want you to meet my future wife," the Duke said, "and she has heard me talk about you."

"I am delighted to meet you, Lady Deirdre," the Sheriff said holding out his hand. "The Duchess has been telling me how much you have done for the Duke since you came North, and as he is a very old friend I can only tell you that I am grateful too."

Before Sacha could reply the Duke said:

"Now listen, Ian, I want your help on two things: first of all, I have dictated my will to my grandmother's secretary, and I want you to witness my signature and make sure it is entirely legal."

"You know I will do that," the Sheriff replied.

"And secondly," the Duke went on as if he had not spoken, "my *fiancée* and I wish to be married secretly in front of you by Scottish Law."

The Sheriff looked at the Duke in surprise.

"Are you talking about Marriage by Consent?"

"Exactly!" the Duke replied. "If I survive being chopped up tomorrow, then the only person who will know about it will be yourself. If anything happens to me, then you will see that my will is observed in the usual way."

"What you are asking is certainly very unusual," the Sheriff said, "and something I did not expect."

"You are really thinking I am a Sassenach," the Duke smiled, "but you forget that through Grandmama I am a quarter Scottish, and that quarter is appealing to you as another Scot."

The Sheriff laughed.

"In those circumstances of course I must agree."

"Very well," the Duke said.

As he spoke he drew off his signet ring and put out his hand towards Sacha. Trembling she put her left hand into his.

He placed the ring on her third finger, then said in a very solemn voice:

"I wish to present to you, Ian Gordon, as Sheriff of this County, my wife, the Duchess of Silchester!"

The Sheriff looked at Sacha and as if he told her wordlessly what to do, she said in a voice that was low and trembled:

"I . . . wish to present to you . . . Sheriff . . . my . . . husband . . . the Duke of Silchester!"

The Sheriff covered their linked hands with his and said:

"According to the laws of Scotland you are now man and wife, and may God bless you and keep you for the rest of your lives together."

The way he spoke seemed to Sacha very moving. She was aware that the Duke felt the same for she could feel vibrations from his fingers joining with hers.

"Thank you, Ian," the Duke said quietly, "and now I think my wife can leave us while we discuss my will, and after that of course, the prospects of the grouse in the autumn."

There was a note of laughter in his voice which told Sacha he was happy, and because she felt exceedingly shy at what had happened she gave the Sheriff a little smile and slipped out of the room.

Only as she shut the door behind her did she hear the Sheriff say:

"Your wife is exquisite, Talbot, the most beautiful person I have ever seen. I do not blame you for making sure of her."

The compliment perhaps more than anything else

brought home to Sacha what she had done, and as she ran to her bedroom to be alone she could only put her hands up to her burning cheeks.

She was thinking it completely and utterly impossible that she was now a married woman, but the ring on her wedding-finger caught the sunlight and told her it was true.

It was difficult to remember that he thought he was married to Lady Deirdre Lang, whom he would marry again when he was well enough to travel South.

All Sacha could think of was that she was the wife of the man she loved, the man to whom she had tied herself, although he would be unaware of it, from now for all eternity.

chapter six

THE Sheriff stayed with the Duke until dinner-time and Sacha therefore had no chance of visiting him as she usually did.

She was disappointed when she learned from Emily that the Sheriff was still there, and all the time she was dressing she hoped she would have a chance of talking to the Duke later.

She did not know quite what she had to say, but she felt now she had taken such an important step as to be married secretly to him it was imperative that they should be together, and she should make sure that it had really helped him before his operation tomorrow.

"I have done it . . . only for . . . him," she told herself.

At the same time it gave her a strangely wonderful feeling to know even though no one else would ever be aware of it, that she was linked to him in a manner that in her dreams would make them one person.

Yet it was not the same as having a Church Service, and her father had often talked of the day that he would marry her.

"I am praying that I shall have the privilege, my dearest," he had said to her a little while ago, "of marrying you to somebody you love and with whom you will be as happy as I was with your mother."

There was a note of sadness in his voice that was always there whenever he spoke of her mother.

Nevertheless, Sacha had been aware that her father was deeply grateful for the years during which he had been happy as few other men are privileged to be.

"I could not bear to think of you married to somebody you do not love," he went on, "and because you are aware of what your mother meant to me and I to her, you know well what a man and woman feel when their hearts are united, and also their souls."

It was seldom that her father spoke so intimately, and Sacha realised that he was talking in this way because something had upset him.

It was only a week later that she learned that the daughter of one of his friends with whom he frequently corresponded because they were both writers, had run away from her husband because he was cruel to her, and had returned home to seek sanctuary with her parents.

"She must have been very unhappy," Sacha said when her father told her about it.

"The marriage was wrong from the very beginning," the Reverend Mervyn replied. "The bridegroom was too old for such a young girl, but her parents were delighted with the match because he was a rich man."

He sighed before he added:

"It is not money or a grand house which makes a happy marriage, it is when two people are joined together by love, and nothing else is of any importance."

"I love . . . the Duke," Sacha said now beneath her breath.

At the same time she wondered what her father would think if she ever told him that she had been married secretly, letting the Duke believe that she was her cousin to whom he was unofficially engaged.

She was quite certain her father would be very shocked and disapproving. At the same time, perhaps her mother would understand.

"I could not risk his life by letting him go for his operation depressed and afraid that I would cease to love him if he was blind, Mama," she said in her heart.

She knew that if she had refused the Duke's request and he died, she would always believe herself to have been a murderess.

When she had her bath, Emily opened the wardrobe doors to ask which gown she would wear.

"They're all so pretty, M'Lady," she said, "that I didn't know which you should choose."

"Then you choose the one you like best, Emily," Sacha suggested.

As she spoke she turned away from the wardrobe, knowing that however beautiful her gowns were the Duke would never see her in them.

Instead he would be with Deirdre dancing in some glamorous Ball-Room under the crystal chandeliers and she would be dazzling him with her beauty as she had dazzled so many other men.

Just for a moment Sacha felt jealous and envious of her cousin then she told herself it was wrong to be anything but grateful, deeply and heart-feltly grateful that she had been able to come to Scotland.

She had the privilege of meeting the most wonderful man who she had thought existed only in her dreams, and to have been kissed by him!

His lips had given her a rapture and a glory that she had thought until now could only belong to the gods.

In her father's book he had written:

"There was a mysterious quivering and beating
of silver wings, the whirring of silver wheels, and
the strange glittering of shining light."

That was what she had felt when the Duke kissed her, and she knew it was what the Greeks had sought and found and which every thinking and feeling man and woman since that time had sought to capture.

"I have been so lucky, so very, very lucky," she told herself, "and it is wrong to ask for more."

And yet she knew she wanted more, she wanted to be with the Duke, she wanted him to kiss her! She wanted to believe that he loved her as she loved him!

Emily broke in on her thoughts.

"Here you are, M'Lady," she said. "This is the gown you should wear tonight, it'll make you look like a breath of spring."

"You are very poetical, Emily!" Sacha remarked.

To her surprise Emily blushed and a deep red flush covered her whole face.

When Sacha looked at her in surprise the maid explained:

"It's me young man, M'Lady."

"So you have a young man!" Sacha exclaimed. "When do you expect to be able to marry him?"

"I don't know, Miss. We'll have to save up for years

before that happens. He writes me poems and while I don't think you'd think much of them, they means a lot to me."

"I am sure they do," Sacha said gently, "and I hope you will both be very happy."

"Thank you, M'Lady, but we has to be very, very careful, seeing as we're working in the same house, with Miss Hannah watching me like a hawk, ready to make trouble if she thought there was anything between us."

Sacha had never particularly liked Deirdre's lady's-maid and she could understand that Emily was frightened of her finding out.

"I am sure you are wise to be careful," she said. "At the same time, I am glad you are happy and you have somebody to love and care for you."

"It makes everything seem different, M'Lady."

Sacha knew that was what she felt, different from what she had ever felt before.

The Sheriff had left before she walked into the Drawing-Room, and the Duchess was alone.

They talked for a little while about the forthcoming operation which would take place the next day, and Sacha learnt that the bedroom next to the Duke's had been prepared as an Operating-Theatre.

The equipment had been sent from Edinburgh, and ordered by the Specialists so that they could have exactly what they needed.

"We are so lucky that Tomkins is such a good nurse," the Duchess remarked, "and looks after dear Talbot better than any woman could do."

Sacha longed to say that she was a good nurse too, and had nursed her father and her mother at different times. They had always said they found her as efficient and more gentle than Nanny.

"Of course," the Duchess went on before she could speak, "you will be able to help Tomkins, which I am sure he would appreciate, although he may be a little jealous of you."

Sacha drew in her breath. Then she said:

"I should have told you before now, Your Grace, that I have to leave the day after tomorrow."

The Duchess looked at her in consternation.

"Do you really have to go South so quickly?"

"I am afraid so," Sacha said. "My parents are expecting me, and everything is arranged for somebody to meet me in London and take me to the station where I can catch the train home."

She thought the Duchess looked perturbed and added quickly:

"Of course I had no idea when I came here there was to be another . . . operation or that the bandages were to be . . . removed."

"I understand," the Duchess said, "and of course you cannot disappoint your parents if they are expecting you. At the same time I feel that Talbot will be upset."

"I have not told him I have to leave," Sacha said quickly, "and I will certainly not do so before the operation."

"No, no, of course not! That would be cruel and might be dangerous."

"But I have to go," Sacha added, "and my maid actually had a letter today saying that everything has been arranged."

Sacha knew the Duchess was surprised that she could not stay, and after dinner when they walked along the passage to the Duke's room, she felt that her attitude was not as warm as it had been before.

'I cannot help it,' she thought despondently, and knew

if it was in her hands she would want to stay at the Castle for ever.

They reached the Duke's room and Tomkins came out to say in his most severe Nanny-like voice:

"I wants His Grace to get his head down as soon as possible, Your Grace."

"Yes, of course," the Duchess replied. "Her Ladyship and I will not stay long. We will just say goodnight."

"That's what I hoped Your Grace would say."

He opened the two doors for them and they went into the bedroom, and as she looked towards the bed Sacha saw that the Duke was smiling.

"How are you feeling, dearest boy?" the Duchess enquired.

"Very happy," the Duke replied, and Sacha knew he was really speaking to her.

"That is exactly what I want to hear," the Duchess answered. "Now Deirdre and I are going to say goodnight because Tomkins insists that you must go to sleep early and have a good night."

"That is what I intend to do," the Duke agreed.

The Duchess bent and kissed his cheek.

"Goodnight and God bless you," she said. "When the Sheriff left he told me that before you go South he is determined to have a day on the river with you."

"He said the same thing to me," the Duke said. "We have a wager of £5 as to who will catch the most salmon."

The Duchess laughed.

"I think you are betting on a certainty. I have never known Ian Gordon to come home with a larger catch than yours!"

"There could always be a first time," the Duke laughed, but he did not sound as if he thought it was likely to happen.

"Then sleep well," the Duchess said and walked towards the door.

Only as she reached it did she look back to say:

"Two minutes, Deirdre. You know how angry it will make Tomkins otherwise!"

She went from the room, shutting the door behind her, and the Duke put out his hand.

"Listen, my darling," he said as his fingers closed over hers. "I have a lot to say to you, but I know what a fuss Tomkins and Grandmama will make if you stay now. Undress and come and see me in about one and a half hour's time, when everything will be quiet."

Sacha's fingers quivered in his.

"Do you . . . think that is . . . something I . . . ought to do?"

"If you are afraid, then I will come to you!"

She gave a little cry of horror.

"No, of course not! You must be crazy! You might hurt yourself."

Then she realised because he was smiling that he had frightened her to make sure he got his own way.

"You will come?" he asked.

"If you . . . want me," she answered. "But if Tomkins finds out . . . he will be angry . . . and your grandmother will be very . . . shocked."

"No one will find out if you are careful," the Duke said. "They will all be careful to leave me quiet and undisturbed."

"Very well . . . I will . . . come," Sacha answered with just a faint tremor in her voice.

He raised her hand to his lips.

"Do not keep me waiting too long," he said. "You know it is very bad for me."

"Now you are blackmailing me!"

"I must talk to you," he replied, "and I am not really speaking lightly when I say that if you do not come it will not only upset me, but I shall certainly try to reach you."

"I think you are behaving very badly," Sacha said, "but I will come for a little while just to...make you...happy."

"That is what I wanted you to say," the Duke replied, and kissed her hand again.

She went from the room and found Tomkins waiting outside.

"Now, Your Ladyship, don't worry!" he said. "Go and have a good night's rest. His Grace couldn't be in better hands."

"I will not worry, and I know how well you will look after him," Sacha said. "I am very grateful."

She gave the valet a little smile as she walked down the corridor to her own room.

Emily was waiting for her to help her out of the pretty gown which she had worn at dinner.

As she did so Sacha asked:

"You have not forgotten, Emily, that we have to leave the day after tomorrow? Mr. Evans told me the time of the train which is early in the morning."

"Yes, I know, M'Lady," Emily replied, "and if we miss it Her Ladyship'll be real angry and so'll Miss Hannah."

"I know that," Sacha replied, "and I have told Her Grace that we have to go."

"I don't mind saying it's made a nice change being up here," Emily said reflectively as she hung Sacha's gown up in the wardrobe, "but I'll be glad to be home again."

"And of course to see your young man," Sacha smiled.

"I'll also have Miss Hannah finding fault, and making me run about like a rabbit," Emily said. "It's bin real nice waiting on you, M'Lady, and it's a pity Her Ladyship ain't as easy."

Sacha did not reply to this knowing it would be a mistake to criticise her cousin to the servants.

At the same time she was well aware that Deirdre could be very difficult if she did not get exactly what she wanted the moment she wanted it, and she was quite certain that Emily bore the brunt of her anger as well as Hannah's.

Then she thought the girl, stupid though they might think her, had a lot of common sense.

"You are quite right, Emily," she said aloud, "and wherever else one has been, it is always lovely to get back home."

However as she spoke she had the uncomfortable feeling that life at the Vicarage would never be the same again because when she left Scotland she would leave her heart with the Duke.

She brushed her hair until it shone like sunshine, and put on one of the diaphanous lace-trimmed nightgowns which had belonged to Deirdre.

She was exceedingly grateful that this and an exquisitely lovely negligee had been included with the other things.

She knew that Mrs. Macdonald and the other housemaids would have thought it very strange if they had seen the plain cotton nightgowns which she wore at home and her dressing-gown which was threadbare and much too short to be fashionable.

Instead she thought in the lace and chiffon negligee with its tiny bows of blue velvet, she looked like a Princess in a fairy-tale.

When Emily left her, before she got into bed she knelt down as she always did at home and said her prayers.

She prayed for the Duke that everything would go well tomorrow, that he would be well and strong again and that his eyes would see as clearly as they had before his accident.

She hoped that when she had gone he would continue for some time at any rate to drink the carrot and celery juice she had persuaded him to take, and also to eat the uncooked salads which the Cook sent up with every meal and which to please her he had eaten also.

"Please, God, let them help him," she prayed.

She knew she had not been mistaken in following her mother's advice because Lady Margaret had helped so many people through the herbs and fresh vegetables she had given them.

There was a large gold clock on the mantelpiece and sitting up in bed Sacha watched the hands of it moving so slowly that she thought time must have stood still until at last the big hand pointed to half past eleven o'clock.

It was then she felt an almost wild excitement surge through her, and while her mind told her this was something she should not do, she knew because the Duke wanted her that nothing and nobody else was of any importance.

"He wants me," she told herself, "and perhaps this is the last time I shall ever be able to please him."

She thrust the thought away because she could not bear to remember that unless she was allowed to see him tomorrow after the operation, which seemed unlikely, this was the last time they would be together.

It would be the last time she would hear his voice, the last time he would kiss her!

At the thought of his lips she felt her heart leap and

she wanted to run as quickly as she could to his room and make sure he was waiting for her.

Then she forced herself to get slowly and quietly out of bed, put on the lace-trimmed negligee, opened the door of her room very, very quietly, just in case there was somebody in the passage.

But everything was silent. There were only a few candles burning in the silver sconces which bore the Macdonald crest, but they gave enough light for her to see her way to the Duke's door at the end of the corridor.

In her heelless slippers she might have been a ghost moving silently over the tartan carpet.

When she reached the outer door to the Duke's room she turned the handle very slowly, half-afraid that after all Tomkins had not gone to bed and was waiting in the small Hall between the two doors.

But there was nothing there but darkness, and after Sacha had shut the outer door behind her she had to grope her way to the second one.

When she opened it she saw that the Duke was sitting up in bed waiting for her, with only two lighted candles beside him.

"You have come!"

His voice was deep and there was a note in it which made her heart start beating excitedly.

"I . . . I am . . . here."

"Pull back the curtains," he ordered, "and tell me if the stars are out and the moon is shining."

She crossed the room to do as he asked.

The casements were open and the stars seemed to fill the sky while the moon was just rising over the moors.

"It is very lovely!" Sacha said in a low voice as she pulled back the curtains of the second window.

"You shall tell me about it," the Duke said.

She moved towards the bed and as she reached it he ordered:

"Blow out the candles, my darling, I want you only to have the light from the stars."

She was surprised, but she blew out the candles as he had asked, and as she did so he reached out to hold her by the shoulders saying:

"Now tell me what you are wearing."

"I think perhaps your grandmother would be... shocked," she answered, "but I have on... only my nightgown... and a very pretty negligee."

She felt the Duke's hands moving from her shoulders round her neck until he found the small pearl buttons which fastened the negligee down the front.

One by one he began to undo them, but Sacha was hardly aware of what he was doing because she was so vividly conscious of his nearness.

In the shadow of the canopy it was hard to see him clearly, and yet she felt as if his vibrations were like magnets which drew her to him, and there was no escape.

Then unexpectedly he pulled the negligee from her shoulders so that it fell to the floor, and as she gave a little murmur of surprise, his arms went round her and he half-lifted, half-pulled her into bed beside him.

She gave a little cry of protest,

"No... please... no!"

But the Duke held her close against him and said:

"My precious, my darling, you are my wife and I want you in my arms, as you are already in my heart."

Because her body was touching his and her head was against his shoulder Sacha felt as if the moonlight was seeping into her as it had done the night before, moving from her breasts up into her throat and to her lips.

She thought the Duke intended to kiss her, and her

mouth was ready for his, her whole being pulsating with a wild rapture that was so overwhelming that it was impossible to think, and she could only feel.

Then as she felt the hardness of his body, she remembered she was only wearing a nightgown and tried to push him away.

"Please . . . we must not . . . I . . ."

"You are mine," the Duke said. "You love me as I love you. God, how much I love you!"

He pulled her close again and now she could no longer struggle but only surrender herself to his strength and his magnetism.

She could feel his heart beating wildly against hers, she thought she had ceased to be herself but was part of the light from the moon.

There was also another light growing in intensity every moment, which came from their love.

The Duke's arms were like steel and it was hard to breathe. Then he said:

"I love you! I did not realise until now that this was what I was always looking for in life only to be disappointed."

"I . . . love you," Sacha whispered, "and when you kiss me . . . it is so . . . wonderful that I feel we are not on . . . earth, but with the gods."

She could not say any more for the Duke's lips came down on hers and she felt his mouth take possession of her and he seemed to draw her heart into his heart and her soul merged with his.

He kissed her lips, her eyes, her small straight nose, and her little pointed chin, before he moved lower to kiss the softness of her neck, giving her wild sensations that she had never imagined.

"No! No!" she whispered because it was so thrilling it was almost a pain.

Then she was not quite aware of how it happened, but he was kissing her breasts and his hands were touching her body.

The light that came from them both grew brighter and more blinding until it was part of the stars and the moon.

"I love you, and I want you!" the Duke said hoarsely. "My precious, my darling, you are mine, and whatever happens tomorrow we have tonight."

Then his lips became more passionate, more demanding, and somewhere far away at the very back of her mind Sacha thought she should stop him, but it was impossible.

Instead there was a strange glitter and shining around them, a mysterious quivering and beating of silver wings and the whirl of silver wheels.

Then there were only the stars, the moon, and the light that shone so blindingly that it became like a leaping fire which consumed them both, and they were no longer human, but one with the gods.

* * *

Much later the Duke said, and his voice sounded very deep:

"How could anybody be more wonderful? But, my sweet, I did not mean this to happen, not tonight, at any rate."

"I . . . love you," Sacha answered, "but I did not . . . know that . . . love was like that."

"What did you feel?" he asked.

"There are no words to tell you how . . . glorious it . . . was," she answered. "There was music and the light that...came from us...both and which was part of the stars...and the moon...and when you...made me...yours we were...gods."

He kissed her forehead before he said:

"That, my precious little wife, is what I wanted you to feel."

"Was it like...that for...you?"

She knew, although she could not see his face, that he smiled before he replied:

"You gave me the perfection which I know I have always sought, but did not believe existed. The perfection of love which is so ecstatic, so compelling, that I am now prepared to believe it is part of the Divine."

Sacha gave a little cry of joy.

"That is...what it is. That is what you made me feel...that what we were doing was...Divine and it could not...therefore be...wrong."

"Of course it is not wrong," the Duke answered. "You are mine, my lovely one, and I will love, adore and worship you for the rest of our lives together."

Sacha drew in her breath.

She remembered that their lives together would end tonight. But she told herself she could not spoil this moment.

Just as she was unable to stop the Duke from making love to her, so she would not spoil something which was so perfect, so pure and so holy that in her soul she knew it had come from God.

"I love you...I love...you," she whispered.

"Tell me again," the Duke said, "but actually, my beautiful one, there is no need for words. You have proved your love as no one else would have done, and I want to kneel at your feet because I worship you."

He did not wait for Sacha to reply, but kissed her very gently as if she was infinitely precious.

Then the softness of her lips made his kiss become more insistent before he said:

"How can you be so perfect in every way? How can you be exactly what I wanted as my wife and as beautiful in your character and personality as your adorable face?"

Then he was kissing her again, kissing her with long, slow, demanding kisses, until she felt shafts of moonlight moving within her again.

And the light was there, glowing more and more brightly so that it seemed as if the moon itself had left the sky to envelop them.

* * *

A long time later Sacha opened her eyes and realised she had been asleep.

As she did so she was aware that the Duke was sleeping beside her.

Her head was on his shoulder, but his arms were no longer holding her fiercely to him and she knew that he was breathing deeply and peacefully with the same happiness that she felt herself.

Now the moon was high up in the sky and it flooded the whole room with its silver light so that she could see his face very clearly.

Even though his eyes were bandaged she knew that he was looking radiantly happy and she was sure there was the same expression on her own face.

It seemed impossible that they could have reached the highest peaks of ecstasy and still be on earth.

For a moment Sacha thought she must kiss the Duke awake so that he could tell her once again in his deep voice how much he loved her, and she would know again the wonder of his kisses, and the touch of his hands on her body.

Then she knew that more important than anything else was that he should sleep before his operation.

Already he had perhaps taken risks with his health by loving her, and yet she could not believe that the rapture they had experienced could harm him in any way, but only give him a greater strength and intensify his will to live.

She looked at him for a long time, pouring out her love towards him and at the same time praying that he would recover to his full manhood.

Then very, very gently she moved away from him and slipped out of bed.

She picked up her negligee which was lying on the floor and stood looking down at the sleeping Duke, thinking of how desperately and completely she loved him.

Then very softly, moving through the moonlight as if she was part of it, she went across the room and let herself out first into the little Hall, then into the passage.

As she shut the outer door, she thought she was shutting herself out of Paradise, never to return.

For one second she thought it was impossible for her to leave the ecstasy and wonder of the man who had taken her up into the sky and shown her the Divine.

'I will wake him and tell him the truth,' she thought, 'and I will tell him how much I love him, and make him marry me instead of Deirdre.'

Then she knew that if she did that she would put the Duke into the dishonourable position of breaking his word and force him into marriage in a way that he would resent and which would perhaps make him hate her.

"There is nothing I can do," she told herself, "except love him secretly, as our marriage was secret, for the rest of my life."

Only when she was in her own room and in bed did she bury her face in the pillow and the tears came slowly and painfully into her eyes.

The Duke had carried her into the sky, but now she was back on earth and she felt as if each tear that ran down her cheek was a drop of blood as if from a crucifixion.

* * *

The following morning when Emily called Sacha she said:

"They've taken His Grace into the Operating Theatre, M'Lady, and Mr. Tomkins is in such a state you'd think he was having the operation himself!"

"It is already taking place?" Sacha asked in astonishment. "Why so early?"

"It's not as early as that, M'Lady," Emily replied. "I came up at eight o'clock, as I always does, but you was sound asleep, so I let you be."

"I ought to have breakfasted with the Duchess," Sacha exclaimed.

"I told Her Grace you were asleep, and she said as how she expected you had stayed awake worrying about His Grace and the best thing you could do was sleep."

Sacha looked towards the clock and Emily said:

"As it's now past eleven o'clock I thought as how Your Ladyship would want me to wake you."

"Yes, of course," Sacha said. "I am ashamed of having slept so late."

She knew in fact she had slept for only a few hours

because she had cried until the stars had faded in the sky and the first golden fingers of the dawn came up over the moors.

It was then she must have fallen asleep and her head still felt heavy and her eyes were swollen from her tears.

She washed them in cold water and hoped the Duchess would not notice. Then she remembered that if she did she would just think she had been crying because she was anxious about the Duke.

Then as she went to the window to look out over the moors the wonder of last night lifted away her depression and she could only think of the Duke's kisses, and the glory when he had made her his in the light which was the light of the gods and the light of love.

"No one can take that away from me," she told herself.

As she finished dressing she walked along to the Drawing-Room to make her apologies to the Duchess, who merely said:

"Do not apologise, my dear. I knew how worried you were last night, and it was the best thing that you should sleep. I knew you will be glad to hear that Tomkins said Talbot had a very good night, and was in such high spirits this morning, laughing and joking with the Specialist, that he might have been going to a party instead of having an operation."

"I am so . . . glad about . . . that," Sacha said.

She never thought the Duke would regret what happened last night, but she was a little afraid it might have been too much for him.

But their happiness had made the Life Force seep through them and she knew her father would have thought it could do nothing but invigorate those who felt it.

It seemed a very, very long time and it was difficult to think of anything but the Duke, until the Specialist who had operated on him came into the Drawing-Room.

The Duchess looked up anxiously as he walked towards her.

"What news, Sir Lindsay?" she asked.

"Very good news, Your Grace," the Specialist replied. "The operation was quite simple and completely successful, and I think in a few days the Duke will find it difficult to remember it ever happened."

The Duchess clasped her hands together and said:

"Thank God, and of course, you Sir Lindsay."

Then as if she remembered he had not met Sacha she said:

"Let me introduce you, Deirdre, to Sir Lindsay Hardwick who has lived up to his very great reputation, and is quite rightly Physician in Ordinary to the Prince Consort."

Sir Lindsay held out his hand.

"I have heard of you, Lady Deirdre," he said, "and how much you helped my patient before I arrived. So I am very glad to give you such excellent news of him."

"And I am very . . . glad to . . . hear it," Sacha replied.

She spoke with difficulty because the relief of hearing that the Duke was all right brought the tears to her eyes.

As if he understood Sir Lindsay said:

"I have other news which I know Sir Colin will bring you very shortly."

"My grandson's eyes are all right?"

"Sir Colin thinks so. He had a look at them while His Grace was unconscious, and the scars have all healed. There is no reason to think the pupils are damaged."

The Duchess gave a little sob as she said:

"God has certainly answered my prayers!"

"What we are going to do now," Sir Lindsay said, "is to put our patient back in his own bedroom, and make

143

sure that he sleeps for the next twenty-four hours. Sleep, as Your Grace knows, is a great healer."

"Yes, indeed," the Duchess agreed.

"After that he will be in Your Grace's hands again, but not I think, for very long."

"I cannot tell you how happy you have made me," the Duchess replied, "and luncheon will be ready as soon as you are. After that I suggest if you and Sir Colin have nothing better to do, the salmon are waiting for you."

Sir Lindsay laughed.

"That is what we hoped you would say. Perhaps you will think it very reprehensible, but we have booked our reserved seats South not for tomorrow, but the day after."

"I should have been very upset if it had been any earlier," the Duchess replied.

While the Duchess and Sir Lindsay were talking Sacha had moved away to the far end of the room to stand at the window looking out blindly into the garden.

She was not only fighting against the tears which threatened to run down her cheeks, but against a mixed feeling of exaltation and misery.

Because the Duke was well and out of danger she wanted to sing a paean of joy to the sky and knew that her love for him was great enough to be unselfish and unselfseeking.

At the same time it was only a few hours before she must leave him, and she knew there would be no chance of speaking to him again: of knowing his kisses or of even saying goodbye.

Tomkins would stand like an angel with a flaming sword to prevent anybody from disturbing his beloved master, and even more effective than any sword was the knowledge that if the Duke could see again tomorrow he must not see her.

"This is the end!" Sacha told herself. "This is where Cinderella leaves the Ball and returns to her rags and cinders with only the memory of the one incredible moment when she had captured the heart of Prince Charming."

Because she could not help it two tears escaped from her eyes and ran down her cheeks and she wiped them fiercely away and managed, when Sir Colin joined the party, to talk quite calmly and sensibly at luncheon.

Only afterwards when the Duchess went to her own room to rest and Sacha went to hers did the sight of Emily packing her trunk make the full misery of leaving sweep over her like a flood-tide.

She could not help wondering if during the night it would be possible to creep in and see the Duke once again. Then she knew it would be a mistake.

If she disturbed him it might do him harm. She also had the idea, which was afterwards confirmed by Emily, that Tomkins would be sitting up with him all night in case he needed a drink or grew restless.

"Like a fussing hen Mr. Tomkins be!" Emily said when Sacha asked her. "He's got the footmen running about fetching this and fetching that! You'd think he was guarding the Crown Jewels of England instead of a sick man!"

"The Duke is more important than any jewels!" Sacha replied.

"I s'pose you're right, M'Lady," Emily agreed. "They thinks the world of His Grace up here, as I expect they'll do at home when they hears that he's going to marry Her Ladyship."

Sacha did not reply, and Emily putting one gown after another into the big leather trunk went on:

"We always thought downstairs that Her Ladyship

would marry Lord Gerard. Ever so keen she seemed on him, and he's more charming than anyone else who's ever stayed at the Big House. But there, I s'pose a Duke's a Duke, and a Lord is only a 'runner up,' so to speak."

Sacha could not help thinking that Emily was far more shrewd than either Deirdre or Hannah thought her to be, but she knew it would be a mistake to encourage a conversation of this sort and she merely said:

"You will be careful, Emily, not to say anything about my being here? You know how angry it would make Her Ladyship."

"And Miss Hannah," Emily added. "Oh, she told me all right I'd be dismissed without a reference, and I'm not so stupid, Miss, as to risk that!"

"No, I am sure you would not," Sacha agreed, "and you have been very helpful and kind, and I am sure everybody is very grateful."

"I doubt it," Emily replied. "But I'd like sometimes, Miss, if I could, to come and see you at the Vicarage."

"But of course, Emily," Sacha replied. "You know you will always be welcome. You must bring your young man to see me. I would like to meet him and tell him how lucky he is to have somebody as nice as you."

Emily's eyes lit up and she said:

"That's real kind of you, Miss. But then they says you are just like your mother and it's the truth."

Sacha felt she could not have had a more sincere compliment, but it was difficult to think of anything except the Duke.

When at last she was able to go to bed, she could only go over and over in her mind the ecstasy and rapture of the night before.

She lay in the darkness knowing she could not bear to see the stars outside and the moon rising in the sky.

She felt that never again would she be able to look out into the night without remembering the silver radiance that had flooded the Duke's room and mingled with the light which came from themselves.

"Now I am crying for the moon," she told herself and tried ineffectually to fall asleep.

She knew that her thoughts, her soul and her whole being was vibrating, yearningly towards the man who was sleeping only a few yards away from her, and perhaps dreaming of her.

chapter seven

As the train carried her South, Sacha felt she was Persephone leaving the sunshine of spring for the darkness of Hades.

While every nerve in her body told her that she was linked with the Duke for all time, her brain told her it was the end and all she could do was to try to live her life without love.

But even to think of him was to revive the sensations of rapture and to thrill again and again to the memory of the ecstatic moment when he made her his and she felt they were enveloped in Divine light.

"I suppose," Sacha ruminated, "many people go through their lives never feeling like this, and I must never forget that I have been lucky enough to know love in all its wonder and glory."

At the same time as the train travelled on there was no comfort in knowing that the Duke thought her to be Deirdre, and it was to Deirdre he would go with the light in his eyes which could now see, and would be thrilled and dazzled by her beauty.

'He will never realise there was any difference between us,' Sacha thought miserably.

If Emily had not been there she would have cried, instead of which she had to exert all her self-control and pride to remain dry-eyed.

As she looked out of the window at the passing countryside all she could see was the Duke, and in the rumble of the wheels all she could hear was his voice saying: "I love you, my precious little wife!"

Sacha had been unable to say goodbye to the Duchess because she and Emily had to leave the Castle at seven o'clock, long before Her Grace would be called.

She had instead, left her a little note thanking her for her hospitality and saying how happy she had been.

She wrote:

"I shall never forget the beauty of the moors and the lights on them, the loveliness of your garden, and the moonlight on the loch."

The thought of the moonlight made her thrill once again as she thought of how it had flooded into the Duke's bedroom as she looked at him for the last time sleeping peacefully in its silver light.

When she finished her letter to the Duchess, Sacha had sat at the desk in her bedroom, wondering if she should write to the Duke.

She could not leave him without sending him some

message since that would make him feel hurt and bewildered by her indifference.

At the same time she was afraid that he might recognise there was a difference between her handwriting and that of Deirdre's.

Their Governesses had often held Sacha's writing up as an example to her cousin saying:

"I cannot understand, Lady Deirdre, why you cannot write clearly and elegantly in the same way as Sacha does. Your writing is sloppy, untidy and often a disgrace!"

Deirdre had merely laughed at the time, but it was so long now since Sacha had seen Deirdre's writing because they had never corresponded, that she knew it would be impossible for her to try to copy it.

She thought for a long time of what she should do, and finally she wrote seven words in the centre of a piece of crested writing-paper printing them in capitals:

"I LOVE YOU WITH ALL MY HEART!"

It was true, so utterly and completely true, that when she looked down at what she had written her eyes filled with tears and before she could prevent it, one fell on the corner of the paper and left a blot.

Feeling she could not bear to write the same words again, Sacha quickly put what she had written into an envelope, and again in capitals addressed it to:

"HIS GRACE THE DUKE OF SILCHESTER."

She left both the notes on the desk, then realising that time was passing she hurriedly dressed and ate the breakfast which Emily had brought her on a tray.

The same servants who had seen her arrive saw her off at the station. Sacha thanked and tipped them and thought as she did so that it was the last time she would be able to be so generous.

Now she and Emily were in a reserved carriage moving South leaving behind the moorlands, the glens, the fir-covered mountains, the rivers and lochs.

Despite the fact that their train was an Express they were late in arriving in London, and Mr. Evans had to hurry them to the other terminus where with only a few minutes to spare, they caught the train in which they were to meet Deirdre.

Emily was more agitated about it than Sacha who was able to remain calm simply because she was beginning to feel that now that she had lost the Duke, that nothing else was of any consequence.

Nevertheless when the train puffed into the station where Deirdre was waiting she felt apprehensive and a little afraid in case anything should have gone wrong.

Then she saw her cousin looking exquisitely beautiful in a very large and spectacular crinoline, and wearing a bonnet trimmed with roses and carrying a bouquet of them.

Lord Gerard was with her and, when they said goodbye to each other outside the carriage, Sacha was aware by the expression in his eyes how much he loved Deirdre, and she was sure that her cousin was looking at him in the same way.

It flashed through her mind that if Deirdre had now decided to refuse to marry the Duke, then she could tell him that it was she who had been with him in Scotland, and perhaps the love he had for her would be greater than his anger at being deceived.

But when Deirdre got into the carriage and the train moved away, she quickly dispelled the little quiver of hope that had arisen in Sacha's breast.

"You are late!" she said sharply as if it was Sacha's fault that this train had also been delayed.

"We only just caught this train by the skin of our teeth," Sacha answered. "The Express from the North was very late indeed!"

"Well, you are here," Deirdre said indifferently.

She put down her bouquet on the seat beside her and adjusted her skirts before she asked:

"I suppose everything is all right, and no one suspected that you were not me?"

Sacha thought it strange that her first question was not to ask how the Duke was, but she replied:

"No one had the least idea. The Duke was operated on yesterday, and another Specialist is removing his bandages today."

"Then it is a good thing you came away," Deirdre said, "or he might have seen you."

She opened the little reticule which hung from her arm and taking out a tiny mirror examined her face in it.

"I have had the most wonderful time, Sacha!" she said. "But we have been getting to bed very late every night, and I am sure it has given me lines under my eyes."

"You look very beautiful!" Sacha said truthfully.

"That is what Henry says," Deirdre replied, "and of course he is right! I cannot see any signs of tiredness in my face, but I shall go to bed as soon as I get home and rest."

"You enjoyed yourself?" Sacha asked.

Deirdre put down the little mirror and replied in a voice which for the first time held a note of emotion in it:

"It has been marvellous! I have enjoyed every moment of the party. I only wish you could have heard the compliments I received."

"I am sure they were very sincere."

"Of course they were, and Harry pays them so eloquently that it is hard at times to believe he is an Englishman, who are usually so tongue-tied."

"I am sure they cannot be where you are concerned."

She was looking at Deirdre wide-eyed and thinking that she was in fact so beautiful that if the Duke saw them side by side he would not hesitate for a moment in supposing that it was Deirdre he was marrying, and Deirdre whom he loved.

When she thought of him holding Deirdre in his arms and kissing her Sacha felt as if a dagger was being pressed into her heart and the pain of it made her put her hand up to her breast.

Because she sighed Deirdre looked at her critically and said:

"I must say, Sacha, dressed in my clothes you look very much better than you usually do."

"It was very kind of you to give me such . . . beautiful things, and I am very . . . grateful."

"You could hardly have pretended to be me in the rags you usually wear! What was the Duchess like?"

"Charming, absolutely charming!" Sacha answered. "She says the Duke is her favourite grandson, and she intends to leave him the Castle when she dies."

"Well, as far as I am concerned, I hope that will not be for a very long time," Deirdre said. "If there is one place I have no intention of going to, it is Scotland!"

Sacha was silent for a moment. Then she said in a voice which she hoped Emily could not hear:

"I am afraid . . . Deirdre, I told the Duke I . . . loved Scotland . . . and thought it one of the most . . . beautiful places I had ever . . . seen."

"That was stupid of you," Deirdre snapped. "You know I hate country-life, whether it is in England or anywhere else."

Sacha paused. Then she said in a low whisper:

"I must see you sometime soon to tell you something you must know before you see the Duke again."

"I suppose I shall have to listen to the stupid things you have said to him, and what sort of trouble you have made for me!" Deirdre said sharply. "Well, there is no hurry, since the engagement party is not for another ten days and I do not imagine the Duke will be coming South until then."

"It is . . . important . . . what I have to . . . tell you!" Sacha insisted.

"All right, all right, do not fuss!" Deirdre snapped. "I will either come and see you, or you can come to me. I will send a groom to tell you which."

She thought for a moment before she added:

"I shall very likely be going to London the day after tomorrow to start collecting my trousseau. There will be some sketches and patterns waiting for me at home, and I am determined to buy a wedding-gown that will be more beautiful than any other bride has ever worn."

She started to talk of the different materials she might choose, and as she became animated and quite pleasant Sacha found it impossible to speak again of the things she had to tell her privately.

It was impossible to say very much with Emily at the other end of the carriage, but Sacha knew although she was terribly afraid that Deirdre would be very angry, that before her cousin saw the Duke she had to tell her how they had been married under Scottish Law.

Because she was nervous Sacha made no effort for the rest of the journey to talk of the Castle or anything that had happened there.

It was obvious that Deirdre was not interested and she continued to chatter about her trousseau, occasionally mentioning Lord Gerard, but otherwise completely oblivious of everything except her own interest and her looks.

When they arrived at the station which was nearest to Langsworth Hall there was a carriage and a brake waiting to convey them and their luggage first to the Vicarage, then on to the Big House.

Hannah appeared from another carriage which she had occupied during the journey and Sacha heard her say to Emily in a vitriolic tone:

"You should've joined me when you stopped at the station to pick us up instead of forcing yourself on the young ladies where you're not wanted!"

"I'm sorry, Miss Hannah!" Emily said looking like a frightened little rabbit confronted by a snake. "Nobody told me that was what I oughta do."

"Your own common sense should have told you!" Hannah said acidly.

Looking crushed Emily walked behind Hannah and as Deirdre stepped into the open carriage, Sacha turned back to say:

"Goodbye Emily and thank you. You looked after me very, very well. I am sure if she had seen how cleverly you managed, Hannah would have been very proud of her pupil."

She made sure that Hannah should overhear what she said, and added:

"Emily was really marvellous, Hannah, and I could never have managed without her."

"I'm glad to hear it, Miss," Hannah said, but she did not sound particularly pleased.

Sacha knew there was nothing else she could do, and as Deirdre was waiting impatiently, she climbed into the carriage to sit beside her.

"You are not to talk to your father of what happened," Deirdre said as they drove off. "The only person who knows where you have been is Emily, and Hannah will deal with her."

"I made you a promise," Sacha replied indignantly, "and you know, Deirdre, that I will not break it."

Deirdre was however, not listening. She was obviously thinking of how successful she had been in sending her cousin to deputise for her and making sure there was no question of their ever being exposed.

"There is one thing I have to tell you, Sacha," Deirdre said in what Sacha thought was a slightly embarrassed voice.

"What is that?"

"Harry said, and of course he is right, that it would be a mistake for you to come either to my engagement party, or to my wedding."

It was what Sacha had expected, but somehow it was a blow to have to put into words.

"It is not that the Duke may recognise you, you know that," Deirdre went on, "but his grandmother might turn up at either function, because of course we have sent her an invitation. I suppose also the Duke will bring his valet with him, and he will have seen you."

"Yes... of course," Sacha said, thinking that Tomkins' sharp eyes might easily see the difference between her and Deirdre.

"And as Harry says," Deirdre went on, "You obviously cannot refuse to come, so you will just have to be ill on both occasions."

Sacha was silent and she continued:

"At the time of the engagement party you can have a bad cold, and on the day of the wedding a headache, or *vice versa*, it will not matter."

"Do you not think... people... in the village will think it very... strange?" Sacha asked.

"Who cares what they think?" Deirdre replied.

There was no answer to this, and a few minutes later they had arrived at the Vicarage.

Deirdre offered her cheek to her cousin saying:

"Goodbye, Sacha, and thank you for being so obliging."

"You will not forget that I have to see you and tell you... certain things I... said to the... Duke?"

She also would have to give Deirdre the Duke's signet ring, though she thought that when she handed it over she would be losing her last link with him.

"I have not forgotten," Deirdre said, "but there is plenty of time."

There was nothing more Sacha could say, and as the footmen climbed down from the box to open the door she stepped out and the carriage immediately rolled away without Deirdre looking back to wave to her.

The Vicarage door opened behind her and she greeted Nanny with a kiss, and as she did so the brake containing two servants and her luggage drew up.

Hannah and Nanny nodded to each other coolly. There had never been any love lost between them.

Sacha's trunks and hat boxes were deposited in the hall and the brake drove away without the menservants making any suggestion that they might carry the luggage upstairs.

Nanny shut the front door with what was suspiciously like a slam.

"Have you enjoyed yourself, Miss Sacha?" she asked. "The Master's missed you, I can tell you that! And so have I!"

"I have missed you too, Nanny."

Only when she went upstairs to take off her bonnet and travelling cape did Sacha remember that she still had some sovereigns left over from the money which Deirdre had given her with which to tip the servants at the Castle.

What she had dispensed had seemed quite generous, and the servants had seemed pleased. But there were, she remembered five golden sovereigns left in her bag.

'I should have returned them to Deirdre,' she thought, 'and I must remember to do so when I see her again.'

This was another reason why they had to meet, but Sacha felt Deirdre was not in the least interested in what she had to tell her, and there was every likelihood of her meeting the Duke without learning what had occurred.

Because that would be disastrous, she thought she had been very remiss in not impressing even more forcefully on her cousin that she must listen to what she had to say.

However it had been impossible in the train to speak freely in front of Emily and the carriage in which they drove from the station had been open.

While she thought it was unlikely that the men on the box could overhear their conversation, Sacha had been too afraid to risk it.

'I will write to Deirdre,' she thought, 'and tell her that as soon as she returns from London, she *must* come to see me.'

159

Then she heard her father's voice calling to her and she ran down the stairs to fling her arms round him.

* * *

Sacha came out by the West door of the Church smiling saying "Good morning!" to the six old people who had constituted the congregation besides herself.

It was an early Communion Service on Sunday morning and the Vicar always hoped that because it was so early, some of those who later would excuse themselves on the grounds of having to cook the Sunday dinner, would find it easier to come to Church before they started.

It was in fact the Service that Sacha enjoyed most, because few people attended it, and this morning there were even fewer than usual.

She always felt as if she was alone there with her father, and the God he worshipped so sincerely seemed nearer to them both when their attention was not distracted by the shuffling of the choirboys' feet, and the fidgeting of those who longed to be out in the fresh air.

This morning Sacha had prayed for the Duke as the sun came through the East window to throw a dazzling light into the Chancel and felt as if she sent her prayers winging towards the glory and rapture of the Heaven into which he had taken her.

She had taken a great deal of trouble in arranging the flowers on the altar, and she put two large vases of arum lilies in the Chancel, which had just come into bloom. They scented the whole Church and were to Sacha a symbol of the beauty and purity of love.

For use when it rained there was a little covered way between the Vicarage and the Church which had been erected by the last Vicar who suffered from arthritis and had to avoid getting cold and wet.

It was shorter than going out through the West door and crossing the Churchyard into the Vicarage garden, but today Sacha wanted to be in the sunshine.

As she passed from the Churchyard into their own garden she undid the ribbons of her bonnet and took it off so that she could feel the sun on her head.

Because it was Sunday she was wearing one of the pretty gowns that Deirdre had given her.

She was very careful with them, and on other days when she was helping Nanny in the house and was unlikely to see anybody she wore her old cotton dresses.

Now as her crinoline swung gracefully and she walked across the unkept grass and up to the Vicarage door, she was wondering if her prayers had somehow found their way to the Duke, and if he was still in Scotland or had come South.

It was eight days since she had left him and in two days time the engagement party would take place at the Big House to which both she and her father had received an invitation.

When she looked at it Sacha had wondered if she dare defy Deirdre and go to the party just so that she could look at the Duke.

'I will not speak to him,' she thought, 'but I could see him.'

Then she knew that would be dangerous, and she could not behave to Deirdre in a way that was dishonourable.

"She gave me the most wonderful experience of my life," Sacha told herself, "and I must always be eternally grateful."

At the same time her heart cried out despairingly for the Duke and every night she wept into her pillow, although she despised herself for doing so.

She had kissed the ring he had given her until she felt she was wearing away the gold.

Then to add to her worries and troubles, Deirdre had not come back from London. When Sacha made enquiries she found that although she had been expected the day before and the day before that, she had still not returned.

She could only hope that she would be at Langsworth Hall tomorrow.

"I must tell her about the secret wedding," she told herself over and over again.

It was not something she could write in a letter, and with Deirdre enjoying herself in London it was impossible to contact her.

Inside the Vicarage she could hear Nanny, who had come back by the quicker route, moving about in the kitchen.

Sacha walked to the door to ask:

"Can I help you, Nanny?"

"There's not much to help me with," Nanny replied tartly. "There's an egg for the Master, and nothing but toast for you. Those lazy hens aren't worth their keep!"

"Toast will be quite enough," Sacha said cheerfully.

At the same time, she could not help seeing a picture of the silver dishes from which she could choose at the Castle. On the table there were always hot scones as well as freshly baked bread, a huge comb of honey besides several jams, and of course homemade marmalade.

'That is the sort of breakfast I shall never have again,' she thought.

She went into the Sitting-Room putting down her bonnet on a chair in the Hall as she did so.

She drew back the curtains to let in the sunshine, then

tidied the cushions of the chair in which her father had been sitting last night.

His latest manuscript from which he had been reading to her lay on a small table beside it, and as she put the pages together in a folder she wished she could read to the Duke what he had written.

It was another of her father's translations from the Greek in which his skill in interpreting and conveying the meaning together with the vivid way in which he used words painted a picture which Sacha thought, was very moving.

She knew that just as the Duke had understood *The Light of Greece* he would also understand and appreciate this book for which she and her father had not yet thought of a name.

'Perhaps it will sell better than the last one,' Sacha thought.

Knowing how much it would please him she wished she could tell her father how both the Duchess and the Duke had appreciated his work.

But she had given her word to Deirdre, and there was nothing she could do about it.

Nevertheless, although she knew she had many other things to do she turned over the pages of the manuscript.

She read again certain passages which she had found so beautiful that she felt they lifted her heart and her mind in the same way that the stars had done when she looked at them through the casements in the Duke's bedroom.

She felt too as if they brought her the light which was an echo of the blazing radiance that had come from the moon and themselves when the Duke had made love to her.

Sacha went on reading until there was the sound of footsteps in the Hall and she realised guiltily that there were things she should have been doing, and anyway her father must now have returned for breakfast.

Quickly she put down his manuscript and as the door opened she turned round with a smile to say:

"It is your fault, Papa! Your book has made me forget..."

Then the words died on her lips.

Coming into the Sitting-Room was not her father in his well-worn cassock, but somebody so tall, so smart, so magnificent that she could only stare at what seemed to her to be an apparition.

Then his dark eyes met hers, and she felt as if the whole room whirled round her and the ceiling fell down on her head, and she knew that she was looking at the Duke and he was looking at her.

For a moment they both stood as if they were turned to stone.

Then as the Duke shut the door behind him and walked slowly towards her, Sacha gave a gasp and in a voice that did not sound like her own, she said:

"I...think you have...made a...mistake and come to the...wrong place. This is the Vicarage...not Langsworth Hall."

"I am aware of that."

His voice was deep, but at the same time Sacha felt that he had not recognised her despite the fact that he was looking at her penetratingly and, she imagined, with curiosity.

Her heart was thumping in her breast, her lips felt dry and it was very hard to speak, but somehow, without looking at him, she managed to say:

"I . . . think you are . . . seeking Lady . . . Deirdre Lang."

"As it happens," the Duke contradicted, "I am looking for Miss Sacha Waverley, as I have something to give her."

"To . . . give her?"

There was a little pause before Sacha was able to say the words.

"I have in fact something which belongs to her," the Duke went on, "and which I think she might miss."

She was so surprised at what he was saying that she glanced at him for a moment, then looked away again.

He was quite near her and she knew, just as she had thought, that with the bandages over his eyes he was the most handsome man she had ever seen, and now that they were removed he was not only overwhelmingly good-looking, but much more authoritative and in a way more intimidating.

She had never imagined a man could be so elegantly dressed, and yet at the same time, seem to fill the whole room with his masculinity.

She knew he was looking at her and it made her feel shy.

She told herself that now he could see her, while he might notice a resemblance to Deirdre, he would know she was not as beautiful as the girl with whom he had fallen in love in London.

Because he was waiting for an answer to what he had said she managed to say hesitatingly:

"I . . . I am . . . Sacha Waverley . . . but I cannot . . . imagine what you have to . . . give me."

It flashed through her mind, and the thought in itself was an agony, that perhaps Deirdre had told him the truth, and he had come to pay her off for her services.

The fact that he might offer her money she knew would not only make her feel degraded, but would also be an abject humiliation.

"What I have to return to you, Miss Waverley," the Duke said formally, "is a book inscribed with your name which I see with interest was written by your father."

As he spoke he held out towards her *The Light of Greece* which Sacha remembered to her dismay she had left in his room when she came away from the Castle.

She had not missed it on her return simply because she had not wished to read again the words she had read to the Duke and which she felt in a way had first drawn them together with a closeness which had turned to love.

As she looked at the book with its worn cover inscribed with her father's name, Sacha remembered he had written on the fly-leaf:

"To Sacha, my dearest and most beloved daughter, who has helped with this book because she believes and seeks as I do for the light which Greece gave to the world."

Slowly Sacha held out her hand and took the book from the Duke.

"Now," he said in a different tone of voice, "perhaps you would be good enough to explain to me how it was that when I could see again, I should find it in my bedroom?"

Sacha searched for a plausible explanation, and she was just about to say that she had lent it to Deirdre when somehow the lie choked on her lips.

She could only look up at the Duke and had no idea how appealing and how lovely her eyes were.

For a moment they could only look at each other. Then he asked:

"Have you missed me?"

"Y . . . yes!"

"How could you do anything so cruel, so damnably unkind, as to go away in that ridiculous fashion without telling me the truth?"

Because he sounded angry Sacha found herself trembling. Then because she had to answer him she said in a voice that seemed to come from a long way away:

"How . . . did you know . . . ? How did you . . . guess . . . or did . . . Deirdre tell you?"

"I think it is I who should be asking the questions."

"Are you . . . very . . . angry?"

"Very angry indeed!"

"I . . . I am sorry."

"That is not enough, not nearly enough!"

"W–what . . . else can I . . . do?"

"There is a great deal you can do, in explaining not only why you tried to lie and deceive me, but also why you were ready to turn me into a bigamist!"

Sacha clasped the book against her breast as if it would somehow calm the tumult within her.

"I . . . I did not . . . mean to do that," she said. "It was . . . just that I was so . . . afraid that if I did not . . . agree to what you suggested . . . it would upset you and the operation might not have been successful."

"I realised that was probably why you did it," the Duke said. "At the same time you should have been brave enough when the operation was over, and I was able to see you, to tell me the truth."

"That is what I would have . . . liked to do," Sacha said. "I wanted to . . . stay with you . . . I longed to stay with you . . . but I had given my . . . word to Deirdre . . . and you are to . . . m—marry her."

"Do you really think I would behave in such a despicable manner?" the Duke asked. "How could you imagine that married to you by the Laws of Scotland I would marry anybody else? There is also the fact that, more important than anything else, I love you!"

The way he spoke made a thrill like silver moonlight strike at Sacha's heart and she felt as if the wonder of it invaded her whole body, and she became vividly and thrillingly alive.

"You . . . 1—love *me?*" she asked in a whisper.

"I love you!" the Duke said firmly. "And as I know you love me, I have come here to ask you what you intend to do about it."

Sacha was trembling as she asked helplessly:

"What . . . can I do?"

The Duke smiled for the first time since coming into the room.

"I think the answer is that you just have to obey me."

As he spoke he pulled her roughly into his arms and his lips found hers.

He kissed her until she felt her whole body merged into his, and he carried her up to the sky as he had done before, and they were one, not now with the soft silver radiance of the moon, but with the burning heat of the sun.

He kissed her until her heart was beating frantically, and she knew his was too, and because it was so wonderful and she was so happy to be with him again that without her being aware of it the tears were running down her cheeks.

The Duke raised his head to look down at her.

"How could you leave me?" he asked. "You are mine,

my darling, as you were when I made love to you in Scotland. Mine now, and for all time."

The way he spoke, fiercely and possessively, almost as if he defied her to contradict him, made Sacha feel as if the sky had opened and she had been swept back into Paradise on the silver wings of love.

"I love you!" the Duke said again.

"But you have . . . promised to . . . marry Deirdre."

The Duke smiled, then put his fingers under her chin and turned her tear-stained face up to his.

"How could you have taken part in such a ridiculous plot to deceive me, thinking that because I was blind I would not know the difference between one woman and another?"

"How did you . . . guess?"

He smiled.

"I admit at first I was bewildered because your voice was sweet, soft and sympathetic, and it was not in the least like Deirdre's. Then, I suppose you would say it was my instinct which told me that the vibrations of your personality were quite different, and that something very extraordinary had happened, but I could not understand what it was."

"I thought I was . . . deceiving you so . . . cleverly."

"As a performance it was lamentable," the Duke replied. "And when you read to me and we talked of Greece, you captivated me in a way no other woman has ever been able to do."

"I am . . . glad," Sacha whispered, "but it was . . . very wrong of . . . me."

"Of course it was wrong," the Duke agreed, "but perhaps my darling, it was meant by fate that your Father's words should draw us together. Once I realised that I loved you as I had never loved anybody before in my whole life, I was only terrified that I might lose you."

Sacha was still for a moment. Then she asked:

"Was that . . . why you . . . married me?"

"Of course it was," the Duke said. "I was not such a fool that I did not realise somebody had taken Deirdre's place at my bedside, and I guessed that it was because she had no wish to waste her time or her beauty on a blind man."

There was a note of cynicism in his voice which made Sacha, because she could not bear him to be bitter, draw a little closer to him.

"What frightened me," he went on, "was that you might try to slip away without my being able to see you doing so, and I would never be able to find you again."

"That is . . . exactly what was . . . planned."

"I guessed that," the Duke said, "but even then I did not realise that having married me you would dare to go on with your deception and, as I said before, label me for all time as a bigamist."

"I . . . I did not . . . think it would . . . matter . . . if you never knew."

"But you would have known."

"I am . . . not important . . . I do not . . . matter."

The Duke looked down at her with a smile on his lips.

"As my wife you are very important," he said, "and as someone I love more important to me than anything or anybody in the whole world."

Sacha gave a little cry.

"That is what I . . . feel about you, but what can we do about it? You have . . . promised to marry Deirdre . . . and I could not bear you to do . . . anything that was . . . dishonourable and would . . . discredit you."

The Duke did not answer. He merely kissed her in a way that made it impossible to think of anything except that she loved him, and that even if he married a thousand Deirdres, one part of him would still belong to her.

Then he said:

"Time is passing, and we have a lot to do, my precious little love, and very quickly."

Sacha looked at him in a bewildered manner and he said:

"Because I am sure it would please you, your father is waiting to marry us again in Church before we leave."

"My . . . father?"

"I have explained everything to him and he understands."

"Did you . . . tell him that I . . . pretended to be Deirdre?"

The Duke shook his head.

"I guessed it would upset him, so I merely said we met in Scotland, fell in love with each other and I am now free."

Sacha drew in her breath with relief.

"But I also explained that it would be embarrassing if our marriage was not kept a secret for a time. Naturally he wants to make sure we have the blessing of God."

"It . . . cannot be true!" Sacha cried, and there were tears in her eyes.

"It is true, my lovely one."

"But . . . Deirdre . . . ?"

The Duke gave a little laugh.

"I have been very clever and I meant to tell you all about it later. But I do not want you to be worried and you will be glad to know that your cousin has refused to continue our engagement."

"Refused? I do not . . . believe it!"

"When you left and I realised what had happened," the Duke explained, "I dictated to my grandmother's secretary a letter to Deirdre's father explaining that following my accident the doctors were not quite certain if I would ever regain my sight. I therefore felt in honour bound to release his daughter from her promise to marry me."

As Sacha stared at him incredulously she asked:

"And . . . Deirdre accepted it?"

"Of course she did!" the Duke said. "You cannot imagine that somebody who considers herself the most beautiful woman in England would wish to be married to a blind husband who will never be able to see her?"

"But . . . you lied!"

"Just a little white lie," the Duke agreed, "to save her pride. I cannot believe she would be pleased if I had told her I was already married to somebody I loved with all my heart and who, in my opinion, is not only much more beautiful than she is, but lovelier than any woman who ever existed, except perhaps for the goddess Aphrodite!"

"That . . . too is a . . . lie."

"No, my precious, it is the truth," the Duke contradicted. "Your cousin is very beautiful—no one could deny that—but her beauty is entirely facial. Yours, my sweet, comes from your heart, your soul, and from what you and I know is a light that shines so dazzlingly that I shall never see any other woman's face but yours."

Because the way he spoke was so sincere Sacha gave a little cry and flung herself against him to put her face on his shoulder.

"There is so much I want to say to you," the Duke said in a low voice, "but, my precious, your father is waiting and I want you to do something for me."

"What is that?"

"I want you to put on the gown that you wore the night when I first kissed you and which you told me was of silver and embroidered with pearls which had the translucence of your skin. That is how I want to see you as my bride."

Sacha raised her head.

"How could you be so...wonderful?" she asked. "How can you think of all these...marvellous things to make me happy?"

"I will answer that question later," the Duke replied. "Now hurry, my darling, and while we are being married, Tomkins, who is waiting outside, will help your maid pack your clothes, so that we can be away from here as quickly as possible."

He smiled before he added:

"There is no need to explain that no one must see you in case it is reported to Deirdre and her father before we are ready to tell them ourselves that not only we are married, but that my sight is not as bad as we feared."

The Duke spoke with a note of amusement in his voice. Then as Sacha stared at him, her eyes filled with love he said:

"Hurry, my darling, Hurry! Or I may be exposed and that, I feel, would be disastrous!"

She gave a little cry and ran away from him across the room.

Only as she reached the door did she stop and pull at a ribbon she had round her neck.

At the end of it was his signet ring which lay hidden between her breasts. She drew the ribbon from it and turned back to hand it to him, warm from her skin.

The Duke took the ring from her and kissed it and as Sacha met his eyes, she knew he was thinking of how he had kissed her breasts.

She blushed and hurried up the stairs to her own bedroom.

As she did so she heard him cross the Hall behind her

and go to the door of the kitchen to talk to Nanny, and as another voice joined in, she knew that Tomkins was there too.

Although she had been home for a week Nanny had not unpacked all the trunks she had brought back with her for the simple reason that they had not yet decided what they would do with the evening-gowns that she would never have a chance of wearing.

The silver embroidered with pearls was on top of the others and as Sacha lifted it out of the box Nanny came hurrying into the room.

"I don't know what you've been up to, Miss Sacha," she said, "but all I can say is that His Grace's the best looking and the nicest gentleman I've met for many a long year, and he certainly knows his own mind."

"I love him, Nanny!" Sacha said simply.

"That doesn't surprise me," Nanny retorted. "He's just what your mother would have wanted for you, and I can't say fairer than that."

As she spoke the tears ran down her cheeks, and Sacha knew they were tears of happiness.

It was Nanny who not only buttoned Sacha into her gown but found her mother's wedding-veil, the orange-blossom wreath, and the fine lace mittens she had worn at her wedding.

When Sacha walked down the stairs, a little shyly, she felt that once again she had stepped into a dream, the fairy-tale which had been so much a part of everything connected with the Duke.

She was half afraid that he might have vanished and was not in reality waiting for her in the Hall! But he stood there, watching her descend the stairs.

There was an expression in his eyes which told her without words how much he loved her, and now she was able to look at him closely she saw there were little white scars around his eyes where he had been injured, but she knew they would fade in time.

It did not detract from his appearance as it might have done if he had been a woman, and she loved each one of them because it was through them that they had found each other.

If he had not been blind, Sacha thought, Deirdre would have gone to Scotland and she would never have met him until after they were married.

As if he knew instinctively what she was thinking the Duke offered her his arm and put his hand over hers.

"Now we shall seek together for the light which your Father understands, the light he will give us when we kneel before him."

Because she knew no other man would have understood so well or said exactly what she wanted to hear, Sacha laid her cheek against his arm with a little gesture he found very moving.

"I love you!" she whispered.

Then she drew him towards the covered entrance which led them directly to the vestry.

No one saw them as they walked from the Vicarage and the Church was empty with the door locked. As they walked to where her father was waiting for them with the sun coming through the East Window behind him, Sacha felt as if the whole building was filled with a blinding light.

They knelt before her father and there was once again the 'glitter and shining in the air, the mysterious quivering, the beating of silver wings, the whirring of silver wheels.'

Then as the Duke put a gold wedding-ring on her finger the light intensified and she knew that they were blessed by God and He had given them to each other for all time.

* * *

Back at the Vicarage when she went upstairs Sacha found that Nanny and Tomkins had filled the boxes she had brought back from Scotland with her clothes, and she had only to change into her travelling-gown and cape.

They put the silver gown in which she had been married on top of the trunk before it was strapped down.

Then as Tomkins lifted it up Nanny ran downstairs to serve breakfast.

"By a miracle," Nanny said as Sacha came into the Dining-Room, where the Duke and the Vicar were waiting, "or perhaps they were giving you a wedding present, those lazy hens laid two more eggs this morning, so there's one for everybody."

She sounded so pleased about it that the Duke could not help laughing.

"I think it is really a unique wedding present, and perhaps the most enjoyable we shall have," he remarked, and the Vicar laughed too.

Because she knew both of them were so happy Sacha said:

"How could I have guessed...how could I have imagined when I had been so miserable this...past week that all the...fairy-tales ever written could...come true?"

"I will make you sure of that, my darling," the Duke said, "and when we can announce that we are married and return to earth from our honeymoon, I would like to talk to you, Vicar, about accepting a living I have on one of my estates in Kent."

The Vicar looked at him in surprise, and he said:

"It carries with it the position of a Canon of Canterbury

Cathedral. This I think would give you more time for writing, which to my mind, and I know Sacha's, is extremely important."

Sacha gave a little cry of excitement.

"Oh, Papa, it sounds wonderful!"

"I think I am dreaming!" the Vicar said.

"That is what I have felt ever since I first met my . . . husband," Sacha said, "and because I am afraid of waking up I hope we will be able to keep our marriage a secret for a long time."

"As that is something I want too," the Duke said, "I suggest we leave immediately. My carriage drawn by four horses is standing outside your front door, Vicar, and could undoubtedly cause gossip in the Village."

"Yes . . . of course . . . we must go," Sacha agreed.

Then as she rose she said:

"Where are we going? I think Papa would like to know."

"I wanted you to ask me that question," the Duke answered. "Tonight we will be staying not far from here at a house I own, but seldom use. From there we will take the train to Southampton."

Sacha looked at him questioningly and he explained:

"My yacht is in harbour there and your father already understands that we intend to have a very long honeymoon and our marriage will not be announced until we return to England."

"It sounds so . . . wonderful!" Sacha said in a low voice.

"I hope you will think so, and I know your father will approve of where we are going."

"Where is that?"

She read the answer in the Duke's eyes before he answered:

"Where else but to Greece? We are seeking the light,

my darling one: the light of which your father wrote so movingly and which you have brought me."

Sacha put out her hand towards him and for a moment they forgot there was anybody else in the room.

Then as she saw the happiness in her father's face Sacha kissed him and having also kissed Nanny hurried outside to where the closed carriage was waiting.

The Duke held back to say to Nanny in a low voice:

"I will give instructions for food and wine to be brought over every week from my estate in Buckinghamshire. You have to give the Vicar strength to finish the book he is writing now and start another."

The expression on Nanny's face was very eloquent but for once she was speechless.

Then as they drove away Sacha flung herself into the Duke's arms and asked:

"It is . . . true? It is really . . . true that we are . . . going to . . . Greece?"

"Of course," he answered. "Where else could we seek the light, and where else could I take a woman who will rival the most beautiful of the goddesses who ever graced Olympus?"

* * *

Later that night in the Duke's arms Sacha asked:

"You are not still . . . angry with me for . . . trying to . . . deceive you?"

"I should have been very angry if I had not been able to find you," he replied. "Even now I can feel the terrible fear that swept through me when I learned that you had gone, and I knew that my grandmother did not understand how desperately afraid I was that I might never see you again."

"It was . . . cruel and . . . wrong of me, but darling I will . . . make it up to . . . you."

"You have done that already," the Duke said, "but I shall punish you, my precious one, by never letting you out of my sight, and by making love to you until it will be impossible for us ever again to be apart."

"I know that already," Sacha said, "and I was so...agonisingly unhappy and so...afraid of the future...without you."

"It was a crazy action on your part, even though I understand that you tried to help your cousin."

He paused before he said:

"I suppose, my foolish one, it never struck you that you might have a baby, and what would you have done then?"

Sacha felt the colour rise in her cheeks.

"You will think me very ignorant," she answered in a low voice, "but I did not know until...after you had...made love to me...how people have...babies."

She hid her face against him and the Duke drew her closer as he said:

"I knew when I kissed you how innocent you were, which again was very unlike your cousin, and when I made love to you it was the most exciting and the most thrilling thing I have ever done in my life!"

He kissed her forehead before he added:

"I also knew it had made you irrevocably mine."

"That is what I...felt," Sacha murmured, "and if you had never...discovered that I was not Deirdre I would...never have married...anybody else because I was...your wife until I...died."

The Duke did not reply. He merely kissed her gently, and yet possessively as if she was infinitely precious.

Then because the softness and innocence of her lips excited him his kisses became more demanding, more passionate.

As he felt Sacha's heart beating against his and he knew that the thrills that swept through her made her quiver he felt his love become a burning flame.

Then the ecstasy of love rose higher and higher to sweep them up into the skies so that they touched the stars and the 'shining in the air' which shone from them both was the light of the gods.

ABOUT THE AUTHOR

Barbara Cartland, the world's most famous romantic novelist, who is also an historian, playwright, lecturer, political speaker and television personality, has now written over 300 books and sold 350 million books over the world.

She has also had many historical works published and has written four autobiographies as well as the biographies of her mother and that of her brother, Ronald Cartland, who was the first Member of Parliament to be killed in the last war. This book has a preface by Sir Winston Churchill and has just been republished with an introduction by Sir Arthur Bryant.

Love at the Helm, a novel written with the help and inspiration of the late Admiral of the Fleet, the Earl Mountbatten of Burma, is being sold for the Mountbatten Memorial Trust.

Miss Cartland in 1978 sang an Album of Love Songs with the Royal Philharmonic Orchestra.

In 1976 by writing twenty-one books, she broke the world record and has continued for the following five years with twenty-four, twenty, twenty-three, twenty-four, and twenty-four. She is in the *Guinness Book of Records* as the best selling author in the world.

She is unique in that she was one and two in the Dalton List of Best Sellers, and one week had four books in the top twenty.

In private life Barbara Cartland, who is a Dame of the Order of St. John of Jerusalem, Chairman of the St. John Council in Hertfordshire and Deputy President of the St. John Ambulance Brigade, has also fought for better conditions and salaries for Midwives and Nurses.

Barbara Cartland is deeply interested in Vitamin Therapy and is President of the British National Association for Health. Her book *The Magic of Honey* has sold throughout the world and is translated into many languages. Her designs "Decorating with Love" are being sold all over the USA and the National Home Fashions League named her in 1981, "Woman of Achievement."

Barbara Cartland Romances, a book of cartoons, has just been published, and fifty-five newspapers in the United States and several countries in Europe carry the strip cartoons of her novels.